WE WERE ON A BREAK

JO LOVETT

First published in Great Britain in 2024 by Boldwood Books Ltd.

Copyright © Jo Lovett, 2024

Cover Design by Head Design Ltd

Cover Illustration: Shutterstock

The moral right of Jo Lovett to be identified as the author of this work has been asserted in accordance with the Copyright, Designs and Patents Act 1988.

All rights reserved. No part of this book may be reproduced in any form or by any electronic or mechanical means, including information storage and retrieval systems, without written permission from the author, except for the use of brief quotations in a book review.

This book is a work of fiction and, except in the case of historical fact, any resemblance to actual persons, living or dead, is purely coincidental.

Every effort has been made to obtain the necessary permissions with reference to copyright material, both illustrative and quoted. We apologise for any omissions in this respect and will be pleased to make the appropriate acknowledgements in any future edition.

A CIP catalogue record for this book is available from the British Library.

Paperback ISBN 978-1-78513-519-4

Large Print ISBN 978-1-78513-520-0

Hardback ISBN 978-1-78513-518-7

Ebook ISBN 978-1-78513-521-7

Kindle ISBN 978-1-78513-522-4

Audio CD ISBN 978-1-78513-513-2

MP3 CD ISBN 978-1-78513-514-9

Digital audio download ISBN 978-1-78513-516-3

Boldwood Books Ltd
23 Bowerdean Street
London SW6 3TN
www.boldwoodbooks.com

To William

1

CALLUM

I'm so shocked that I can't speak; all I can do is stare.

Approximately thirty seconds ago, I felt like the luckiest man alive. I was too hot and my feet were pinching from semi-jogging three miles across Rome pulling a suitcase, but when I rounded the corner into this street and saw the camper van parked at the opposite end, I was practically euphoric.

I need – *needed* – this lift. Flights across Europe are grounded indefinitely due to ash from an unpronounceable Icelandic volcano. I *have* to get back to London, and this is apparently my only option. So, I was desperate for it.

Now, though...

Now I'm wondering whether I might need a hole in the head more than the lift.

Because now I can see the woman who offered me the lift.

I'm so stunned that all I can do is keep on bump-wheeling my case across the cobbles towards her, my eyes focused on her face, with my mind and my mouth... not working.

I come to a halt a few feet away from her.

To give my brain a rest from trying to process what's in front of me, I focus on the pale blue van behind the woman. It's parked haphazardly – diagonally half-on, half-off the pavement, between an overflowing skip and a motorbike – but is clearly well-loved, with its shiny bodywork and cheery flowery curtains.

My eyes switch back to the woman herself. She has dark brown hair tied in a high, thick ponytail, she's tanned and she's wearing a green mini-dress and gold flip-flops. Very Emma.

She is, indisputably, her.

'Emma,' I state. The way the two syllables come out of my mouth sounds very odd, like I'm trying out speaking for the first time ever.

'Callum?' she replies. Genuinely. Like that. Like it's a question.

I just continue to stare. And then she begins to stare too.

I'm staring because she's *Emma*.

And she's staring in a way that indicates that she thinks she might recognise me but she can't one hundred per cent place me yet. Which I think I would find extremely offensive if I weren't busy thinking – in weird slow motion – *what the actual...*

I carry on staring while, with what feels like a huge effort, I rewind things in my mind.

Emma and I didn't speak in person when we agreed this lift; we just messaged. It was literally just words to the effect of *Hi, I hear from Azim that you need a lift back to London; yes I do, thank you so much; no worries, let's meet tomorrow at eight thirty, I'll send you the address; thank you again, I'll pay for fuel, you're a lifesaver.*

Emma seemed rushed, and I was busy on a client dinner that Janet, one of the executive assistants at my law firm, had set up for me, so I wasn't keen to chat either.

All my friend Azim – who'd put us in touch – told me was that Emma was mint (his word), and I trust Azim.

Azim knows a lot about me, including, broadly, the fuck-up

that my life was before we met at law school, but he doesn't know the specifics. Emma was a specific.

I know from the contact details he sent over that he has her saved in his phone as 'EM', which I assumed was 'Em', but now I realise might also be 'Emma Milligan'. I wonder what he has me saved as. Clearly not with my surname, or Emma would presumably have realised that I'm me.

Azim told me that Emma's a good friend of his wife, and is in Italy on a road trip following a big break-up with her ex. Which is fine. The ex thing. Obviously there is no reason that she shouldn't and wouldn't have had boyfriends since me. I mean, it's been twelve years. Of course she has. I mean, I've had other partners. Of course she has too. My slight feeling of – I don't know what, surely not jealousy – is entirely irrational. Due to shock, obviously.

God, though.

I cannot share this journey with her.

Twelve years is a really, really long time, and I am entirely over her, obviously, but equally, Emma was my first, maybe my only, love, and it nearly killed me staying away from her. I don't want to sit in an enclosed space together for sixteen hours. I clearly have moved on from her, because I lead a happy, functioning, *great* life, but I don't, I realise, want to know how she's been or what she's like now. I don't want to be reminded. I don't want to have any flashbacks. I just want to keep on moving forward with my nice, happy, Emma-free life.

I do, however, really need to get home.

When everyone was sending me *'Mate, you've done so well landing yourself a free extended break in a luxury hotel in Rome'* messages, all I could think about were all the things I have on in London, not Rome, in the coming week.

I have at least five important in-person work meetings, and, crucially, an appointment with a gold-dust plumber to have the leaking tap in my kitchen fixed. The plumber's part of a highly successful women-only plumbing company and she has a nine-week waiting list. I need to be there when she arrives because last time she came, I was out, and my neighbour, who had recommended her, slept through the doorbell, and that was that. The tap still leaks and the drips still stop me getting to sleep and the tiles underneath are getting wrecked (and I still had to pay the one-hundred-and-ten-quid daylight-robbery call-out charge). I've tried and failed to find another good plumber and I *need* her.

I also have Azim's daughter's christening at the end of next week and I have to be there because I'm a godfather.

And most importantly of all, I need to get back to Thea; I can't be away from her for too long.

I do therefore very much want to go home.

Maybe I don't have to go with Emma, though. Maybe she isn't *really* my only option.

An image of Janet comes into my head. Janet is always right. This morning, for example, as predicted by her, there were apparently no free taxis in the whole of Rome, hence my three-mile sprint.

One of her last messages yesterday was:

> Your ONLY hope is to find a car share with someone who does not mind your VERY INCONVENIENT lack of driving licence.

(Janet can be very emphatic.) She went on to reiterate the lack of trains, boats, coaches, taxis, and non-driver car shares, and the total lack of response to her registration of my plight with the hotel reception, the British embassy and all online sites. She also told me that she'd fruitlessly explored buying a car and paying a driver.

On my side I messaged literally everyone I know asking about friends of friends who might happen to be anywhere near the Rome area and heading for London.

Janet's view is that I'd be insane to pass up a lift, even if it's in an ancient camper van. She thinks Emma is my only option.

She's obviously right.

So either I stay in Rome indefinitely or I grow up and deal with spending two days in a van with someone who is in fact just an ex from a very long time ago. That's all.

I can absolutely do it. I was being irrational before, from shock.

Of *course* I can do this.

I googled the journey yesterday. It's sixteen hours on the road, which I'm guessing will be two eight-hour days. There's no need for us to talk beyond basic pleasantries. We don't have to eat together this evening or tomorrow morning. We don't even have to stay in the same hotel. It will be absolutely fine.

I can definitely do this. Definitely.

As long as Emma's happy to.

2

EMMA

No. No, no, no, no, no, *no*.

It *is* him.

Even though it's unimaginable that the Callum I knew – *my* Callum – could possibly have turned into this smooth-looking man – I mean, he's wearing a navy Ralph Lauren shirt, the smartest pair of dark jeans I've ever seen, brown suede loafers (possibly Prada) and an insanely tidy haircut – it *is* Callum Harding. I know – *knew* – the bones of him *so* well, and his face is older but it is still him. The same impossibly square jaw and deep green eyes and gorgeous, perfectly arranged, slightly imperfect features.

It's him.

I have offered to drive Callum Harding all the way back to London.

As in the two of us alone together in the van for days and days.

I can't do it. Certainly not. No, no, no.

I feel myself frowning as I try to work out how this has even *happened*.

I think back to the call from Azim. When he asked if I could give a friend of his called Callum a lift, I told him *No problem*, because of course I'm happy to help a friend of a friend. Very, very stupidly I did not say: *What's his surname and did I ever spend two years joined at the hip with him?*

Azim is my very good friend Becca's husband. Becca and I met just after Callum and I had our on-a-break split (which turned out to be permanent without either of us ever acknowledging it). She and Azim met and got married in a real whirl quite recently, while living in New Zealand, and I only met Azim after they arrived back in England, with their gorgeous baby, Rose, in tow. I liked Azim immediately and trust his judgement, and obviously I trust Becca.

Azim said Callum was a really good friend of his from law school.

Law school? Callum? Although to be fair he does now look very lawyer-like.

Azim told me that Callum is very sensible, very sober, very clean-living and very hard-working. I'm pretty sure he used those exact words.

My Callum Harding was none of those things.

Azim also described him as mint and someone who would never take advantage of a lone female in a camper van, and to be fair those things *do* apply to my Callum Harding.

But going back to the sensible, sober, hard-working *lawyer* thing... I mean, no.

Do a slim-fit Ralph Lauren shirt and suede loafers lie, though?

I don't know. It really is incomprehensible. But anyway. Here we are. Staring at each other in a back street in a not-very-fancy neighbourhood in Rome.

From the way Callum's eyes are on stalks, his Adam's apple's moving but he's making no sound and he's gripping his case white-knuckle hard, I'm certain that he recognises me. Which of course he does; unlike him I have not morphed into a completely different external persona. I wonder for a split second whether he *knew* he was getting a lift with *me*, and then I realise that, no, of course he didn't. If he'd ever wanted to get back in touch there are wiser ways of doing it. A quick coffee on neutral territory for example would be a lot better than several days of close proximity far from home. Plus, he'd have to be an amazing actor to fake the speechlessness and wide eyes.

We have been staring at each other for a very, very long time.

'How are you?' he asks eventually. And, yep, that's Callum Harding's voice. Deep, with a slight Scottish accent that I love. Loved, I mean.

How am I? Erm, shocked and pissed off.

'I am *good*,' I say, surprised that my voice is working. 'How are you?'

I realise that I do mean the question. I have – obviously – thought about him from time to time (quite a lot) over the years. I might also have googled him a few times (quite a lot) too, but there are a *lot* of Callum Hardings and I've never found him. Maybe because I did not know that my search should include the words *neat and tidy-looking lawyer*.

'Also good,' he tells me. 'Thank you.'

It's weird. It's like watching an actor that you've always seen in similar roles suddenly playing someone completely different. Like Ewan McGregor not being the *Star Wars* person but the dad in the second *Nanny McPhee* film. Very confusing.

His voice is the same, though. Although entirely sober and somewhat horrified. I'd never heard him sound horrified until the last time we spoke. That last time stuck with me.

'Great,' I say, and then we resume our staring, until I remember the traffic and the fact that I hauled myself out of bed way earlier than usual to make sure we wouldn't get stuck in the Rome rush hour.

Most of me wants to get into the van and drive off without

Callum. A tiny part of me, I realise, wants to know everything about what he's been doing for the past twelve years. How my Callum turned into this version of himself. Mostly, though, I really do just want to run away from him and not go there again.

'Sooooo.' I produce a really big smile that I do not feel. 'I need to get going.'

'Of course.' He smiles back. When he used to smile at me when we were young, the smile always started in his eyes before his lips moved. Now his lips just go kind of sideways and back again. It annoys me that just *thinking* of how much I used to love his real smile makes my stomach lurch a bit. 'I really need to get back to London. And I have no other options. I fully, fully appreciate—' he sounds both incredibly earnest and fairly miserable, which, ridiculously, I find quite cute '—that you probably *really* don't want to travel with me, but I'm kind of desperate, so if you're still happy to have me, I'd be incredibly grateful for the lift.'

Dammit.

I do not want to spend several days with him.

I do not want to spend even several *minutes* with him; I'm already feeling all stomach-churny, heavy-shouldered miserable as memories swirl around my mind.

What can I say, though?

All the news channels have been saying that flights could be off for weeks, and if I'm Callum's only option and he's desperate to get back…

'Of course.' Clearly, there is no other answer I can give. 'I'm all ready, so shall we go, so we don't get caught in the morning rush hour?'

'Great. Fantastic. Thank you so much.'

This is so weird. If you discount the past twelve years of not seeing each other, we've gone straight from mutual horror that we've split up for at least the time being to mutual horror that we're going to be sharing this trip for the next four days. And that is just odd.

At least we can have breaks from each other when we aren't driving. We don't even need to stay in the same place overnight. He could book a hotel if he can afford it. And never judge a book by its cover but his super-smart clothes and shoes do indicate that he *could* afford it especially given that his travel is now very cheap. (In the only text we exchanged beyond the very basic he said in very strong terms that he couldn't accept the lift if I wouldn't let him pay for fuel so I agreed to let him pay half, but that won't be much compared to a flight.) Okay so I'm cheering up a bit. Four hours' driving a day isn't long. We have twenty other hours to be apart each day.

Who am I kidding. Four hours is a *long* time to be stuck together.

Okay, no, it isn't. It will be *fine*. We can listen to music. And not talk. All good.

'Wonderful,' I chirp insincerely. 'Maybe put your suitcase at the back there.'

I point and then climb up into my seat at the wheel.

Before he gets in, I ask, 'Been to the loo?'

Callum raises an eyebrow – I'm guessing because he wishes to point out that he's an adult.

'I'm sorry,' I say, 'but the number of fully grown men who say they don't need to go and then within half an hour are *desperate*.'

He can go in my hotel. (That's a strong word for where I stayed last night but it does have loos and checkout time was not until eleven.)

His eyebrow is still half-raised. 'Yeah, no, I'm all good thanks – on the bathroom front.'

I give in. 'Okay, cool. Soooo... let's go?'

Callum's still standing in the road. 'Your shoes?' he says.

'Shoes?' I look round. Have some of my shoes fallen out of the van?

He's looking at my feet. 'Just thought you might have forgotten to put your shoes on.'

'No?' I wiggle my feet. 'I'm wearing shoes.'

'You're wearing flip-flops.'

'Flip-flops are shoes?'

'Not *driving* shoes, though?' He's frowning slightly.

'I drive in flip-flops all the time.'

'Really?'

'Yes, really.' Honestly.

'Just that I'm pretty sure that it's illegal to drive in flip-flops?'

'What? Really? Why?' I hear my voice go quite high and realise that I'm frowning myself now. This is a ludicrous conversation. I've driven hundreds if not thousands of miles in flip-flops without mishap.

'Because they could get caught on a pedal and cause an accident.' He's definitely serious.

I think of a loophole. 'Is that just a British law, though?'

'Maybe. It's sensible, though.'

I stare at him. This is just *weird*. Callum is lecturing me about being sensible.

For some reason, I continue to engage.

'The thing is, it is a very hot day.' Satisfyingly, I see him nod. I deliver my crunch blow. 'And the van doesn't have air con and it is not safe to drive when you're boiling hot, so I'm actually being *safer* wearing flip-flops to drive.'

'What?' he asks.

'Yep,' I confirm. 'I am right. And I am not changing my shoes. Are you getting in?'

'Right. Okay.'

Callum hefts his not-that-small suitcase into the back of the van effortlessly and even through his shirt I see his biceps flex. A little flashback of naked Callum pops into my head. I blink and look away quickly, even though he obviously doesn't *know* that that's what I was thinking.

It's really weird how thinking about his much younger naked self feels quite *rude*. Like I'm being intrusive. And that is just odd.

Oh my God.

He remembers me naked too. Well, I say that. He was so out of it so much of the time that maybe he doesn't. Plus, maybe he's had so many partners since that we've all merged into one.

Okay, and now I'm annoyed at that thought. Really I'm being quite ridiculous.

Callum closing the rear door and climbing up next to me is a welcome interruption of my thoughts. Although I immediately realise that it's also a very unnerving interruption. Callum, in all his largeness, is now sitting in the front of my van next to me. If I change gear too flamboyantly my hand might bang against his leg. I'll need to be careful.

His voice cuts into my thoughts. 'Thanks again. I really am deeply grateful. Can I help in any way to improve the journey? Map reading? Provision of mid-journey snacks?' He looks at the – admittedly old-fashioned – dashboard and adds, 'Help with tuning the radio or switching the wipers on?'

'The radio doesn't totally work,' I tell him. 'So I use my phone.'

About the windscreen wipers, there's no need to tell him that there are basically none (there was an incident with a low-hanging tree a couple of days ago, which ended up with one completely broken off and the other one not working) so we can't drive in the rain. But it doesn't matter because no rain is forecast along our route for the next few days and as soon as we get into France I'll get them fixed, so he never needs to know.

Actually, maybe I *should* have told him they're broken; he might have decided not to come.

I open my mouth to say it and then close it again. He doesn't seem happy to be here either; he's clearly only joined me because he's desperate to get back, so there's probably nothing I can say to get rid of him, other than *piss off out of my van* (I *wish* I could say that) and this new Callum incarnation seems strangely big into OTT adherence to road rules (I mean the flip-flop thing – *weird*), so it would be better to say nothing.

So I tell him, 'Google Maps help and snacks would be lovely, though.'

I suddenly frown. Why did he ask what he can do to help but not offer to share the driving? Also, I'm pretty sure that Azim said that he doesn't drive.

'Azim said that you don't drive? That you don't have a licence?'

'Yeah,' is all Callum says.

Does he not remember that I was there when he passed his test? I mean, he must do, surely, because it led to our break-up. Which, despite subsequent events (or lack thereof), was definitely huge for him too. He *must* remember it, surely.

He got *really* drunk the night of the test. I had to take his keys and hide them so there was no possibility of him driving. He was *so* stupid then.

And the thought of him being his stupid self but with the ability (and apparently the inclination) to drive terrified me, and was part of the reason I ended up giving him an ultimatum: he had to stop the drinking and the insane alcohol-induced wildness. We both cried a lot when I said that, and then he told me he'd prove himself to me immediately.

From there we started our 'on-a-break' split, and then... he never got in touch again.

He *definitely* passed his test.

But now he's saying he doesn't have a licence.

I kind of want to ask what happened, but also I really don't. There's no good story that I can think of behind someone having a licence and then losing it, and, really, that's the whole reason that Callum and I aren't living in suburbia right now with our two point five kids, a couple of cats and maybe a goldfish. His wildness. Other than that… I mean, I thought we'd be together forever. I'm guessing he did too. That would be why he proposed.

'Okay, then,' I say, and put the key in the ignition.

3
___

CALLUM

Emma turns the key right and left in the ignition as the engine sputters and... does not start.

I watch her tut at the van – as if it's a living creature rather than an inanimate object – as she continues to turn the key.

I'm pretty sure she was thinking about asking me why I no longer have a driving licence. I'm very glad she didn't; that is not a conversation I want to have with her.

It doesn't seem as though the engine's going to start.

I'm almost mesmerised by her slim hands on the key. When the engine fails to catch yet again, the *whoops* expression on her face tempts me to smile despite myself and I wonder whether I might be a lot better off if the van doesn't start after all. I do not need to revisit the way I felt when we split. Maybe staying in Rome until flights are back on is the lesser of two evils.

Yep, maybe I should just get out now and walk away. The engine thing must be a sign. Revisiting the past is rarely a good thing; it certainly wouldn't be in this case.

I could walk. I could *hitchhike*. Why didn't I think of that before? Why didn't *Janet* think of that? Is she losing her touch?

I open my mouth to say *thank you so much but actually goodbye* just as the engine finally gets going and we lurch up and down.

'Oops, the handbrake. Every time.' Emma releases it and sends a half-smile in my direction as we lurch again, but forwards this time. And then we're driving down the street, narrowly avoiding bins and bollards on either side, and I guess my decision's made.

And, no, really that's fine. We split up *twelve years* ago. We're both adults now. I'm a completely different person from the one I was then. Emma's obviously lived a lot of life since then too. We – I – can do this.

My mind veers back to the driving licence thing, and I decide that I need some distraction, because I really don't want to go there.

'Music,' I say firmly.

'Music?' Emma's keeping her eyes on the road, which I have to say I'm pleased about, because the van seems quite tricky to manoeuvre and we're still in what seems to be a maze of narrow streets overhung with tallish, terraced houses, washing hanging from balconies, the occasional fruit and veg stall that we come far too close to, and people hurrying about the beginnings of their days.

'What would you like to listen to? Favourite radio station?'

'The radio doesn't totally work,' she reminds me. She stops and clunks the van into reverse because the corner we're trying to get round is very tight. She leans to look in the side mirror on my side.

'Would you like me to move that for you so you can see it without straining?'

'No,' she almost shrieks as I reach for the handle to roll the window down. (This van looks like it dates from decades before electric windows kicked in.) I raise my eyebrows and she says, 'Sorry, that might have sounded like an over-reaction but please don't touch that mirror. It falls off sometimes and it's a nightmare to get it fixed.'

'Oh, I see.' Not a surprise given the unreliable engine and not-totally-working radio.

'Honestly, it's actually a great van,' Emma says as she reverses again because we still aren't round the corner.

Something I know about her that I doubt will have changed: however much she doesn't want to talk or she's upset or whatever, she can't help herself, she still chats. Like I can tell she's about to do now, despite clearly not being too happy to be sharing this journey with me.

'It's the bones of the vehicle that count, not the fancy extras,' she continues.

'That is true,' I agree politely. 'I've seen a lot of *Top Gear*. My nephews love it. You can cross entire inhospitable deserts and tundras in vehicles like this.'

I was going to say *worse than this* but I realise that that probably isn't true.

'Exactly.' Emma finally has the van round the corner and we're back to dodging bollards, people and the occasional stray dog.

I look at Google Maps again, keen to get out of the city and properly on our way as quickly as possible.

'Left here,' I say.

Emma keeps going straight.

'I can't go in there,' she says. 'Limited traffic zone.'

I look up from the phone. 'This is a dead end, though.'

'Yep.' She's already embarked on turning round.

'Bloody *hell*,' she says as she finally gets the van all the way round after an eleven (maybe thirteen) point turn. 'That was a *tiny* turning space.'

I look over my shoulder at the not-that-small space and maybe I snigger slightly.

'Sorry, would *you* like to do it?' she grumbles. 'Or can you not actually drive due to lack of licence? And weren't you the person who directed us into the dead end in the first place?'

'Both very fair points,' I acknowledge, her mention of the driving licence reminding me that nothing about today is funny.

She shoots me a small I-got-you-back smile and I find myself swallowing because it gets me in a way that I don't want to think about.

'How's the map reading going?' Apparently she hasn't noticed that her smile made me feel... I don't know, weird.

I blink and then collect myself and look at Google Maps again.

'Yeah, no reception here,' I say. 'This has no idea where we are.'

'Okay, I'm going to keep driving until it finds us.'

The ensuing driving around and fruitless where-are-we-going discussion are good in the sense that they're a distraction from where I think my thoughts might have been going.

Eventually we're in a street with slightly lower buildings and a better signal.

'We're literally one road away from where we started.' I point at the phone. 'And we've been going for forty minutes.'

We have to turn left into a very narrow road with very tall buildings because it's no right turn, and we're back to no reception.

'Google Maps has us again,' I finally say after more seemingly aimless driving around. 'Right, left, second right and we'll be onto a main road.'

'Perfect,' she says while I think about how much more time we've wasted. I'm really hoping we're going to be sticking to motorways and main roads for the rest of the trip, otherwise at this rate we'll be going into a third day on the road.

Fifteen minutes later, we're still queuing to turn into the enormous line of traffic on the main road.

'It's obviously full rush hour now,' Emma says, not sounding remotely upset. 'I quite like traffic jams,' she adds – more of the chat she cannot help herself starting.

'What? Who likes a traffic jam?' Turns out I can't help engaging.

'They've very low stress,' she explains.

'In what way?'

'You aren't going to have a crash when you're in a jam, are you? And you don't have to worry about changing lane and doing roundabouts and stuff.'

'But you're only in your car because you want to go somewhere. And once you get going you're still going to having to do the lane changing and roundabouts.'

'In the *moment*, though, it's nice. You can just watch the world go by.'

'More fun doing that in a café with coffee and cake, though?' I suddenly register the more salient point of what she said. 'Are you...? Do you...?'

I don't want to be rude but how novice a driver do you have to be to find roundabouts so stressful that you'd rather sit in a traffic jam? Hasn't she just been on a big road trip?

'When did you pass your test?'

'In April, a couple of weeks before I left for this holiday.'

Wow. It's July. So she's been driving for three months. That is... not long. Although, obviously, she's got a lot of miles under her belt now, and the van's bodywork looks great so she's clearly had no mishaps to date.

So all good. I'm very lucky to have this lift and we will obviously get back to London in one piece.

'Oh my goodness, what's he doing?' Emma points to where a man's just driven from behind us down the wrong side of the road, thus blocking entry to where we need to go, and is trying to turn out into the traffic. The driver next to him opens his door wide, scraping the other man's car, and they both get out and start yelling and gesticulating. A couple of other drivers get out of their cars and join them, followed by a couple more, and soon it's total chaos. They move round the corner onto the main road, where more drivers join in.

Emma leans forward, her forearms on the steering wheel, her eyes dancing, looking like she just needs popcorn and she's all set for as long as the show lasts.

I'm a lot less happy about being stuck here, but somehow, as she laughs and then rolls down her window to talk in extremely minimal but surprisingly effective Italian to a woman standing next to the van, I find myself almost enjoying the whole thing.

And then Emma says, 'Are you coming?' and gets out and walks off down the road.

I do not want to join her. This is ridiculous. It's getting hot, there are fumes everywhere, this is a *work* day, for God's sake. I don't want to get involved in mass road rage in a not-that-nice neighbourhood of Rome. Except Emma's now in the middle of it. Literally: she's standing in the middle of the group, now gesticulating at least as much as everyone else.

I really don't want to but I'm going to have to join her. I can't just leave her in the middle of a huge multi-person argument.

I'm back with the speed-walking (my shoes are feeling a lot better now, at least) and am next to Emma very quickly, just in time for her to say, '*Alora, en el coche,*' while she points at the man blocking the street. I think that's Spanish, not Italian, and the man's face is thunderous, but clearly something about her manner works because to my, and – from the dropped jaws around me – everyone else's astonishment, he grumbles himself back into his car and begins to reverse, people scattering out of his way.

'Nice,' I say to Emma as we walk back to the car.

'That was *nothing* compared to my day job,' she tells me, and I realise that I have no idea what she does for a living. Twenty-four-year-old me wouldn't have believed that I'd have no idea what path Emma's life would take.

I nearly ask and then I hesitate, because I do not want to get involved at all. I don't want to know what she does. I don't want to know anything about her. I just want to get back to London and go back to not seeing her again and hardly ever thinking about her any more.

I do want to know, though, I realise, and again almost ask. But then I remember that I was supposed to be keeping my distance from her during this journey and I feel like we've already been talking too much.

So instead of asking what she does, I say, 'Well you've done a great job here. The queue's actually moving.'

Which is true, so we hustle ourselves fast back into the van and crawl forward until we manage to turn right. For a woman who hasn't been driving that long, Emma has great skill in regular lane-swapping to take advantage of ebbs and flows in the levels of traffic, and we're making a lot better progress than everyone else.

'I thought you loved a traffic jam because you don't like lane changing?' I can't help but ask.

'Yep.' She's looking intently between her rear-view and side mirrors and does another sudden lane switch. 'This requires too much concentration. It's very unrelaxing.'

I decide not to point out that we *could* just sit in our own lane like you're supposed to, because from my perspective the more distance we cover, the better.

'So, music,' I say, because it's kind of weird to sit in total silence but we definitely shouldn't talk too much. 'What would you like?'

And then I add, 'If you would like music,' because I don't want to impose. Maybe she likes driving in silence.

'I have a...' she begins. Then she stops for a second, before finishing with, 'I'm really very easy. Whatever you like.'

I wonder what she was going to say and then realise that maybe she was about to tell me that she has a playlist for journeys and then realised that she doesn't want to share that with me. I get it. I wouldn't want to share mine with her either. Too personal. You're giving away a lot about yourself with your playlist.

Silence, though. Music would be better.

'What about starting with some eighties greatest hits?' I suggest. She always used to love eighties nights.

'I can never say no to eighties music.'

'I know.' That was awkward; why I am referring to the past? 'Let me search.'

And soon we have eighties greatest hits blaring out of my phone and this is good. Emma could be anyone, just a woman I happen to be sitting in a van with listening to 'Last Christmas' in the middle of July.

About four songs in, Emma starts singing along. If she's anything like she used to be, I'm surprised it's taken this long; she always used to sing to everything. She never learns the actual words, just sings *la*.

I find myself joining in, with the actual words, because I know the actual words.

'Oh my God,' I suddenly say, halfway through Emma blasting out *la* at full volume to 'Karma Chameleon', a song that all people everywhere surely know the words to. 'Remember when you did the miaow thing?'

She read something that said if you sing *miaow* when you don't know the words no one can tell and it works way better than *la*. It was not true.

I should not have reminded her. She immediately switches from *la* to *miaow*, before cackling with laughter.

'No, please no,' I say.

We carry on with the la-ing from her and the actual words from me as we make our way out of Rome and onto the motorway. Singing-wise, we're a match made in heaven or a match made in hell, depending on how you look at it, because she has the tune and I have the words.

I can't help looking over at the speedometer fairly regularly. We're getting overtaken by literally everyone. And that is because we are driving at about forty-three miles an hour.

'I think the speed limit's probably at least 110 kilometres per hour.' I google as I speak. 'Actually, it's 130 on the motorway and it looks like it's 150 sometimes. That's *fast*.' I google again. 'That's 93 miles an hour.' I look back at the speedometer. I don't want to be rude but... 'So if you liked, we could go faster,' I suggest.

'I don't *love* driving that fast,' Emma tells me, tapping the steering wheel in time to 'Bohemian Rhapsody'. 'It's stressful.'

I nod. It's her decision, obviously. And I don't fancy going hell for leather in a vehicle this rickety, so fair enough. Equally, though, I'm pretty sure we'd be safe going at, say, sixty miles an hour, and we'd get back a *lot* faster. Google Maps isn't basing its estimates on people going at half the speed limit, is it?

'I totally get that,' I say, 'but I'm just wondering whether we should go a little faster, so that we cover a bit more ground while the going's good?'

I see Emma glance down at the dashboard and she says, 'Oh, yes, sorry.' She then puts her foot down and we reach the heady heights of fifty-five miles an hour.

I do a surreptitious calculation on my phone. We could still just about get back in two days going at this speed; we'll just need to do maybe ten to twelve hours' driving a day. Which I'm guessing

Emma will be happy with because it isn't like we have anything else to do along the journey.

* * *

Half an hour later, I'm beginning to feel okayish about this trip. We haven't exhausted the eighties greatest hits yet and we have several other decades to go through plus themed lists; we can absolutely listen to music the entire way and not really talk, other than polite necessities, and then we can go our separate ways. I won't have missed much in London and it's nice to have seen Emma and confirmed that she seems fine, and so all good from my perspective; I hope that everything's good from hers too.

The skies have been growing gradually greyer over the past few minutes and it's started to spit. I have to fight with myself not to mention that Emma hasn't yet turned her windscreen wipers on, but I shouldn't interfere; some people obviously find the wipers more distracting than the raindrops.

As the rain picks up, I do find it hard not to wonder when she's going to put the wipers on, though. I mean, I can barely see anything through the waves of water sliding down the windscreen so she must have equally poor visibility. This cannot be safe.

'So annoying,' Emma mutters, just as I'm about to suggest (maybe beg if I'm honest) that she turn the wipers on. 'It doesn't look like it's going to stop. How far until the next exit? Is that a sign? What does it say?'

'I don't know because I can't see out of the window because of all the rain. Maybe the wipers would help?'

'They don't work. Well, *it* doesn't. There's only one left. We need to turn off.'

The rain's pelting down now, like someone's chucking swimming-pool-sized buckets over us from above, and visibility is poor to non-existent.

To her credit, Emma's slowed to a complete crawl. To her discredit...

'What were you *thinking*?' I find myself shouting. 'How long have they been broken?'

She mumbles something.

'What?'

'I didn't think it would rain,' she says, still mumbling. 'I do check the weather forecast very regularly.'

'Italy isn't the desert, though?'

'Summer, though?'

I apply huge willpower and don't shout any of the many other obvious things that spring to mind, because I don't want to take any of her attention away from the road.

Because of the direction of the rain, we can actually both see out of our side windows and fortunately we come to an exit within a minute or two. Emma's still not catching my eye at all and I'm still struggling not to be *really* annoyed. She could *die* driving like that. *And* this is going to hold us up for who knows how long.

After a few minutes of crawling along narrow, windy roads where we can't safely park, we come to a clearing off to the left, which looks like a car park nestled amongst some trees.

Emma parks us in there and we both look around.

There's a canopy of trees above us, so thick that it's fairly dry underneath. I get out to take a better look and to make sure that I don't shout at her about what was she *thinking*: you can't go on a motorway trip with non-working windscreen wipers.

There's a big board on the opposite side of the clearing. I don't speak Italian at all but I think it's showing some walking trails and naming some of the plants along the way. I pull my phone out. No signal. Okay, so no way of seeing where we are, what the rain forecast is, or where the nearest windscreen-wiper-fixing garage might be. Right.

Emma emerges from the van, stretching her arms and legs.

'Sorry, sorry, sorry.' She does actually sound pretty contrite. But then she continues, 'I always check the weather forecast a lot, obviously, and honestly this was a big surprise. We were probably due a break, though, so no bad thing.'

I stare at her. Does she *mean* what she just said?

I should not engage. I should walk round the clearing, maybe walk down the lane to see if I can get a signal. I should not ask her what the actual hell she is talking about.

I really shouldn't.

But, 'Sorry, what?' I hear myself say. 'The weather forecast isn't infallible, is it? You're very lucky not to have had a crash before now. Plus, it's quite soon for a break. We're going to go into a third day of travel at this rate. Do we not need to find a garage as quickly as we can and then get ourselves straight back on the road?'

'Obviously I *am* going to get the wipers fixed because obviously yes, it is dangerous but I thought since it wasn't going to rain at all while we're in Italy I might find a garage in France because I speak French and I don't speak Italian. And also I don't want to disappoint you but we're definitely going to go into a third day of travel. I would say a fourth or even fifth. It's a really long way.'

'It's not that long?' I query, incredulous. 'Google Maps says sixteen hours' driving.'

'I can't drive that far in one day.'

'I...' I don't know where to start. I look at her beautiful, still-so-familiar, but also now in many ways quite unfamiliar features. I don't know whether I want to shout at her or shout at myself or just walk away.

For the time being, I decide that shouting is a bad idea.

'I'm going to go and see if I can get a signal on my phone,' I tell her.

'Okay. I have an umbrella. Let me find it for you.'

'I'm good, thanks.'

As I walk out of the clearing and down the lane, I wonder whether I should just keep on walking, right back out of her life.

4

EMMA

As Callum marches himself away from me (hooray), I take my own phone out, and if I'm honest can't help smirking a bit when I see that, unlike him, I have reception (four bars).

I should call him right now (or as soon as he's moved enough to have reception) and tell him, so that he doesn't have to walk too far in the rain.

He must already be soaking, though, so a little bit more rain won't make any difference. And he's clearly *really* annoyed with me so I'm sure he could do with the walk. Plus, it's very weird being around him and I would like a little (long) break from his company.

I'm switching between three different weather forecast apps and they're all telling me that this rain is set in for the rest of the day. (I cannot *believe* what an idiot I was to assume it wouldn't rain; Callum's obviously right about forecasts being unreliable and it being ridiculously dangerous to have no windscreen wipers in a downpour.)

I need to make a plan and I'd rather do that without Callum here so I can think straight.

Also, I want to think about Callum because something's niggling at me.

So I'm going to take his lack of phone reception as a gift and sit down on a log – lovely and dry due to the tree canopy – and enjoy some blissful Callum-free peace and quiet.

The log's surprisingly comfortable actually, and it's extremely peaceful here, definitely conducive to good thinking.

Practical things first: are we anywhere near a garage and, if we aren't, are we anywhere near a hotel?

It looks like the nearest garage is about ten kilometres away. It would have to be *really* close, I realise, for me to be able to drive safely there right now. Outside this cosy forest shelter it's bucketing down; in fact some of it's even starting to seep in here through the branches above, and, going by how dry the ground is, even beneath the bed of brown needles at my feet, that isn't something that happens very often. So basically I can't drive anywhere without new wipers and I can't get new wipers until it stops raining.

Or can I? Maybe I could get a taxi to the garage. But could someone from the garage transport all their wiper-fixing tools here? And would it cost a fortune to pay them to come out? It would still probably be less than the cost of an extra night in a hotel, though.

It looks like there are a couple of small hotels about three or four kilometres away. That's quite a long way to carry a bag in this weather, and there's the cost of an extra night added to the trip to consider. Except I really don't fancy camping here by myself and I really don't fancy camping here with Callum. Walking in the rain would be better and I'd pay good money to avoid him.

I stretch my legs out in front of me and stare at my feet. I like the colour I painted my toenails yesterday. I was choosing between an orangey one and a greeny-blue one. I went orange and that was a good decision. By contrast, my decision to wait until getting to France to get my wipers fixed was *bad*, as was my decision to agree to give a lift to a person who I thought was just a friend-of-a-friend called Callum.

Okay, so maybe my best approach is to see if I can get a taxi from here to the garage and from there to a hotel if they can't fix the wipers. I wonder if you can get Ubers in the middle of the countryside an hour outside Rome during a European-wide no-flight crisis.

I'm going to have to wait for Callum to come back, I realise, or at least call him and tell him that I'm going. Otherwise when he gets back here he might think something terrible's happened to me and call the police or something.

Having Callum with me is definitely the worst part about this.

I mean, okay, yes, if I'm *actually* stranded in the middle of nowhere there are people (my mum, my sister, my friends, basically everyone I know) who would say that it's a *lot* better for me to have Callum around *just in case.* (Honestly, when you embark on a trip like this there's a *lot* of 'just in case' chat from people who care about you, which is obviously lovely but also a teensy bit annoying at times.)

However, I have not been enjoying his company today.

He was the love of my life. Until I met Dev. Who I think I thought had become the love of my life until he asked me to marry him and I realised that I couldn't imagine pottering around a garden and doing crosswords and hopefully still having sex with him when I'm eighty, so I said no very regretfully and we broke up.

When I think about it, it never felt as breathtakingly all-consuming with Dev as it did with Callum, but that's probably – almost certainly – because I was a lot older when I met Dev. Obviously you don't love – or think you love – someone in the same way when you're more mature. I probably wouldn't fall in love with Callum in the same way now had we only just met.

Anyway, I don't like being with him. It took me years to get over the feeling that I was somehow incomplete without him in my life and, even though overall he seems *very* different from how he used to be, he's also the same in some ways. Like his smile. And his face. And his bigness. And the little edge to his voice when he's being sarcastic. And the fact that (when he's sober) you feel like nothing can really go wrong when he's there.

Apart from maybe having your heart broken.

And on the heartbreak point, something very, very horrible is starting to creep into my mind and solidify as an actual thought. I thought we really loved each other and I have memories of us together as the perfect love. We didn't break up because we didn't love each other any more; we broke up because I couldn't deal with Callum's *wildness* any more – I was terrified that he'd do something terrible to himself – and he couldn't stop with the wildness.

These thoughts – memories – are starting to cause a very twisty feeling in my stomach, almost physical pain, because they're leading to something that has been quite nebulous in my brain since I first realised this morning that Callum was *Callum* and looking like a completely different Callum from the one I used to know.

He's a lawyer, according to Azim, as in he holds down a job with regular working hours and presumably turns up every day when he should do and is sober when he turns up. And presumably he no longer does things like staying out for three nights in a row and turning up on a beach in Barcelona when his mother thought he was at his cousin's house in Edinburgh, drunk and dressed head to toe in a stranger's clothes, or accidentally investing his (not very big) life savings in a two per cent share of a llama farm in Poland, or taking a job as a sushi chef after pretending he'd grown up in Japan and being fired on day three. (Surprised it took that long.)

Or trying to drive off in a stranger's car while very drunk the day he passed his driving test, which was our last big argument. After that, the next day – the last time we saw each other – we didn't argue, we both just got sad.

I'm guessing that his lack of licence now might relate to an occasion when he didn't have me there stopping him doing something terrible while drunk.

He isn't drunk now, though, is he. *Now*, he's really annoyed because my van does not have working windscreen wipers and that's *dangerous*.

He's right. It is obviously very dangerous to drive in the rain without working windscreen wipers and I was stupid not to get them fixed immediately. *However*, he's being very hypocritical given what he tried to do driving-wise when we were young.

I'm like whatever about the hypocrisy, though.

What I am now about to admit to myself, which I'm really upset about, is that I really, really believed – and still did until today – that we loved each other as much – almost more than – anyone could ever love anyone else. We split up because he was destroying himself and he wouldn't get help and I couldn't bear to see it and he didn't want me to see it. And when in desperation I gave him a clean-yourself-up-or-we're-done ultimatum, he said fine, I'll see you again when I'm sorted.

And that was that.

And I waited. And waited. Because I really believed that he would sort himself out and that he would come back to me.

I never changed my number or my email address.

He never came back.

And until today I just thought that he must be living some out-of-control life somewhere and that I'd never see the Callum that I thought he could have been – the one who would have been my life partner. I didn't actually ever think that version of Callum could exist in this universe.

Basically, I acknowledge to myself as I kick a pile of pine needles and then regret it when some get stuck between my foot and the bottom of my flip-flop, I am deeply hurt that he got clean and then clearly chose to make his new, clean, functional life *without* me.

The fact is: it turns out that sensible, sober Callum didn't love me.

Which should be *fine*. Water under the bridge. It's all *way* in the past.

I am hurt, though, I think as I shake my flip-flop to get rid of all the pine needles still sticking to it, and then put it back on and start walking round the clearing. I'm sick-to-the-stomach, unable-to-raise-a-smile, life-feels-suddenly-incredibly-empty level hurt.

As I reach the board that Callum was looking at, I can't help thinking that I'm more upset by this than I was by my split with Dev.

It isn't because I loved Callum more though, not really. It's just the youth versus maturity thing. Probably everything feels bigger when you're young and you don't know how to deal with your emotions; that's all.

The board is not that interesting. We're in a national park and it's got trails and stuff. It is not going to be taking my attention away from my thoughts.

I don't want to be wallowing in what-might-have-beens or my-first-love-did-not-love-me-as-much-as-I-loved-him thoughts.

I need to phone a friend. Solitude is unhealthy.

I choose Samira, because she was there through the Callum years and the just-post-Callum years so I won't need to explain anything to her.

'Ems.' Just hearing her voice is good. 'Don't tell me, you're somewhere amazingly beautiful in Italy while I'm sneaking a fag break in a really smelly alleyway where I might get murdered any minute.'

'You should put the cigarette out and go straight back inside.' I'm already feeling a bit better just from hearing her voice. My *friends* are my reality. Callum is just a weird blast from the past. That's all. 'What's your weather like?'

'Weather? Actually very nice and sunny today in London, so I'm genuinely not going to be jealous about yours.'

'Rightly so because here it's raining more heavily than I've seen for a very long time and I don't have working windscreen wipers so I'm stuck in a forest in the middle of nowhere and I can't go anywhere.'

'Emma, genuinely that sounds more dangerous than this alleyway. Are you in your van? Don't wander around by yourself.'

'No, honestly, I'm fine.' In a minute, when I'm feeling fully normal, I'm going to tell her about Callum and then I'll feel much better and then I'll send Callum a text telling him that I'm going to a garage and then I'll call a taxi.

Hmm. I've just realised that Callum must have changed his number because I still have his old one stored in my phone and when we arranged me giving him a lift, the texts came from a different one.

Well, there you go. I waited for him and I did not change my number, while he moved straight on and changed his.

'Ems?' Samira's been talking, I realise, and I have very rudely been caught up in my Callum-thoughts.

'Sorry, bad line,' I fib. 'What did you say?'

'Are you in your van with the doors locked?'

'Well, no, but it's fine.'

'Are you entirely by yourself in this forest, though? Like, are you with a trusted companion?'

I look around me. Samira's paranoia on my behalf is getting to me. Callum could be anywhere, miles away by now.

'How do you know there isn't a murderer behind some trees waiting to pounce?' she continues. '*Get back in the van.*'

'Okay, yes, I'm getting in right now.'

I love Samira but I wish I'd phoned someone more blasé. She's been worried about me this whole trip and once someone else tells you that you should be scared it's hard not to feel a little tinge of worry. I mean right now of *course* there aren't any lurking murderers but also I am a tiny bit panic-stricken.

'In the van yet?' she asks as I fumble the key. (The van dates from way before remote-control keys were invented.)

'Yep. I...'

'Hey.' A man's voice comes from the other side of the van and I find myself screaming. Really, really blue-murder-level screaming.

'Emmmmmmmmaaaaaa.' Samira's screaming too.

'Emma?' Oh. Callum has appeared from round the van. 'Are you okay?'

He's sounding quite panicky, as you would if you heard someone screech like that.

'Yes, fine, thank you.'

'Emma?' Samira's still fairly screamy at her end of the phone.

'It's okay,' I tell her. 'I'm with a... friend... and he'd gone to use his phone and now he's back and you'd got me into a terrified frame of mind so I screamed but it's fine.'

'What friend? I heard a man's voice? Have you *hooked up* with someone?'

'No, no, no hooking up.' I do not look at Callum as I say that. 'Just giving a lift to a friend of a friend because of the volcanic ash downing the planes. He needed to get back to London and we were both in Rome.'

'Okay so I can see two scenarios playing out here,' Samira tells me. 'One, he's a murderer. Two he's gorgeous and you fall in love.'

'I mean, three, he's a perfectly nice man who does not murder people but with whom, I—' I cannot talk about not falling in love with Callum when he's standing right next to me because that would imply that I do feel that there's a possibility that I will fall back in love with him (which I certainly will not do), which would obviously be an excruciating conversation to have in front of him '—just have a perfectly amicable journey and do not see again.'

I glance at Callum and see that he is staring hard at a tree trunk just to his left. He's clearly aware that someone is questioning me about my travel companion. A wave of sadness washes over me for a moment as I think that in the past he would have been outright laughing at me at this point but obviously now he feels too awkward to do that.

'Is he single, though?' Samira persists. 'And attractive?'

I actually do really want to tell her it's Callum and that I *hate* this situation, but I'm definitely, definitely not going to say it while he's standing next to me.

'Don't know and average,' I say airily. 'Anyway, got to go. Got to deal with my windscreen-wiper situation. Speak later.'

'I see you have reception here,' Callum notes as I end the call.

'Yep.' I didn't look properly at him while I was speaking to Samira but now I register that he is unbelievably sodden.

Drops of water are literally dropping off his eyelashes and nose and earlobes and it is genuinely comedic. I find myself beginning to laugh even though obviously that is not polite or very sympathetic and I shouldn't.

Also, I note further: his very thick, dark, curlyish hair is not totally wet through because it's so thick the water hasn't penetrated to the underneath bit, and now the top has started to dry and is curling a lot at the nape of his neck and on top. Basically, it looks very, very cute.

I'm not laughing so much now; I don't want to look at him and think he's cute.

I shift my gaze down and oh my goodness that was a mistake. His shirt is not as thick as his hair and is *entirely* soaked through, and even though the fabric is dark, his *extremely* nicely muscled chest and stomach are outlined in a very Mr-Darcy-coming-out-of-the-lake-in-the-1990s-version-of-*Pride-and-Prejudice* way and I'm *really* not laughing now; instead I'm blushing like nobody's business.

Okay. So I need to stop this. Apparently I am ogling my soaking-wet ex of many years ago while he is just irritated that I didn't mention that I have reception.

'I was about to phone the nearest garage and ask if they would be able to come here and replace the wiper,' I say, in my best business-like manner, keeping my eyes firmly away from his chest. 'It's too far to drive there in this and it looks as though the rain's going to continue for a while.'

'I already phoned them,' Callum says. 'They can't come until tomorrow because they finish early on Mondays. They need us to drive there. Which clearly we cannot do.'

'Oh.' I frown. 'Maybe there's another garage.'

'I asked one of the executive assistants in my office to call around and she couldn't find anyone who can do it today.'

'Oh,' I repeat. This is not welcome news. I was totally pretending to myself that it would all be fine and someone would come and do the wipers and we'd make it to Florence today as planned. 'There must be other garages. I'll call a few more.'

I open up Google Translate and type *'Would you be able to come to a forest to mend my windscreen wipers?'* but Callum shakes his head.

'Obviously you're extremely welcome to check and I could be wrong,' he says, 'but also I don't think I'm wrong.'

'Maybe it's worth a shot, though.' I just don't want to be stuck here with Callum.

More water drips off him.

'The van's open,' I say. 'So if you want you can get a towel from your bag.'

'I don't have a towel. I was staying in a hotel.'

'Oh yes. Let me give you one of mine.'

'No, no, it's fine, honestly.'

I look at him. He's got the set-jaw look he always used to have when he was going to refuse to listen to me. Usually when I was trying to be the voice of reason. Unless he's changed a *lot* there's no point trying to argue with him when he's in this mood and this is not a battle worth having because he's a grown man and he's going to feel disgustingly damp all day at this rate but he'll be *fine*. Plus, I recall, my towels have all already been used by me because I'm on my way home and didn't want to do any more laundry.

'Okay,' I say, and start phoning garages.

Ten minutes later I have confirmed that Callum was completely right. We're stuck here until tomorrow at the earliest unless the rain stops.

I walk over to the edge of the clearing to peer up at the sky.

Yup. It's very grey and the deluge is showing no sign of letting up.

'I guess we should both find a hotel, then,' I say when I get back to Callum where he's still standing next to the van. His clothes and hair are a little bit dryer-looking now but he must still be feeling very uncomfortable.

'I also checked out the hotel options,' he says. 'And taxis. And they aren't that great.'

'How un-great?'

'No taxis at all, probably because of the volcanic ash situation, and only one hotel within walking distance and it looks quite... basic. I'm guessing a lot of tourists have had to stay on because of the flights.'

'I don't want to be rude, but I might just phone a couple of places myself.'

Another ten minutes later I have established that Callum was again completely right. Given the constraint of having to get anywhere we go on foot, we both have two options. Camp in or out of the van, or go to the one hotel there is within five kilometres.

I have also established something beyond ridiculous, like fate is *trying* to set us up in true clichéd rom-com style.

I decide to tackle it head-on.

'There's only one room in the one hotel,' I say.

'Yup.'

We are not sharing it. Obviously.

'So you're soaking wet and you have no towel so you should take the room,' I tell him.

'While you...?'

'I'll stay here.' I try not to gulp as Samira's doom-laden warnings come back to me. It's all nonsense. I'll be fine if I stay in the van and lock the doors. Oh, God, what if the murderers have *tools*? It's definitely easy to break into the van; I've done it myself twice (with a bit of help) when I've locked the keys inside. Okay, no, that's an easy problem to solve: I'll stay awake all night. No, but then I might go to sleep at the wheel tomorrow. Oh *God*.

'This is a tricky one.' Callum frowns a little under his drying curly hair. Ridiculously, the frown somehow just makes him look even more gorgeous. It kind of adds a moody edge to the handsomeness. 'I don't want to be sexist and I obviously have no right whatsoever to dictate to you. But I would be very worried about you if you stayed here alone. So it looks like if you insist on staying here I'll have to stay here too.'

I stare at him in horror. A whole twenty-four hours or more just the two of us in the van? No.

'Outside the van, I mean,' he says, hurriedly. 'You in, me out.'

'Well, we can't do that,' I say. 'You're wet and you'd freeze or go mouldy overnight and I mean just obviously not.'

'So you have to come to the hotel.'

I stare at him in more horror.

Then I decide just to say it.

'But we can't share a room.'

'No,' he agrees. Thankfully. 'I'm thinking we go to the hotel and we explain and there's bound to be a communal area where I can sleep and just use the bathroom in the room. If that's alright. When you aren't there.'

'But that would be very uncomfortable. No one likes sleeping in a chair.'

'You have to drive tomorrow and I don't.' He smiles like he's just played a huge trump card, and to be fair, he has. 'I can snooze on the journey.'

I'd be quite happy if he snoozed, actually. People can't talk or be sarcastic while they're snoozing.

'Maybe, then,' I concede.

'Shall we phone back to confirm our booking and then get going now?'

'Okay.'

'Let me pay?' Callum holds out his hand for the phone.

'No, no, my treat,' I say. *Treat* is not the right word. 'I'm the one who stupidly did not have working windscreen wipers.'

'I mean, you *are* the one who stupidly did not have working windscreen wipers *but* you are also doing me a huge favour.' The expression on Callum's face does not indicate that he's currently receiving a huge favour; he actually looks like he's just discovered that he's trodden in something quite grim. 'And I would very much like to pay.'

'Half each?' I suggest. I don't like the whole being paid for by a man thing.

'Oh, for God's sake,' Callum slightly snaps. 'Without you I'd be completely stuck in Rome. As it is I at least have the *possibility* of getting back to London sometime this week.'

'Okay, er, thank you,' I say eventually.

'Right. Good.' Callum pulls his phone out.

'Wow,' he says when he gets off the line. 'The price.'

'Eek. What?' I'm imagining thousands and thousands. And I'll be honour-bound to pay half and be bankrupted but at least we'll have a lovely bathroom and Callum will hopefully have a lovely sofa to sleep on.

'Twenty-two euros,' he says.

'Oh wow.' My not-that-nice hotel in Rome was nearly eighty euros a night and we aren't that far outside the city. 'Well, on the upside I don't feel guilty any more that you're paying.'

By unspoken agreement we take it in turns to get our overnight bags out of the van. I don't want to get mine at the same time that Callum gets his, because I don't want to inadvertently touch him, and from the wide berth he's giving me I'm guessing that he feels the same way.

'Should you lock the van?' Callum asks when we're at the edge of the clearing with our bags.

'I was just about to,' I lie, and then go back and do it. It's hard to remember everything when your whole day's gone so spectacularly tits up.

And then I go back to the edge of the clearing and take the

handle of my wheelie bag and we stride out into the driving rain to begin the utter farce that is a three-mile walk towards one very, very cheap hotel room to be shared with the ex love of your life.

5

CALLUM

The great news about the way the heavens are emptying their guts onto us is that the crashingly loud rain prevents us from hearing each other speak, so we just can't talk.

As I take the occasional glance at Emma squelching along next to me, I can't decide how I feel. Angry? Nostalgic? Bereft all over again? Impressed that Emma had an umbrella and has managed to keep it from blowing inside out the whole time and that her flip-flops are clearly in fact the right footwear for this because it's like we're wading through a stream?

I do know that I'm incredulous. As in, how can we – I – possibly be in this ridiculous situation?

Emma stops and says something that I can't hear, and then points left down an even smaller lane than the one we're on. She's been guiding us the whole way via Google Maps from under her umbrella and I just have to hope that she's good with directions. I try to remember whether or not she used to be when we were together and realise that I just don't know; we didn't really do a lot of wholesome activities like country hiking.

After a few more turns it becomes apparent that Emma can

indeed read a map on her phone correctly, because we're standing outside the hotel.

We follow signs to the reception through an archway into a courtyard with a sheltered passageway all round the outside.

'This is like cloisters when you visit an abbey or cathedral,' Emma says.

'I think this *is* an old abbey.' I point to all the intricate stone carvings on the pillars around us, and the church-like building opposite.

We come to the reception and I say, 'Maybe I should wait out here.' I can't politely go inside anywhere when I'm as wet as this.

Emma looks at me and clamps her lips hard together as though she's trying not to laugh, and then after a couple of moments says, 'Yes, maybe that's best.' She definitely laughs as she goes inside without me, and fair enough.

The door to the reception is a huge, ancient-looking, solid oak one, but I can just about see her through a little window to the side, and she's doing a lot of gesticulating and nodding. She checks something on her phone and my own phone vibrates very shortly afterwards.

I extract it with difficulty from my sodden pocket and discover that Emma has sent me a message. It says:

> FYI: I had to say we're married. Don't think sleeping in the communal area is a goer.

I'm about to reply with a lot of question marks when the door opens and Emma emerges, followed by a monk.

'Hello... darling.' Emma does some absolutely ridiculous grimacing and eye-rolling at me with her back to the monk. 'This is actually a monastery and the very kind monks very kindly allow guests to stay in some of their rooms, the last one of which you booked, and this lovely man, Father Davide, speaks English.'

'Please don't worry about dripping on the floors; they are all stone. We are delighted to welcome you,' Father Davide tells us in excellent English as we walk along the far side of the cloisters from where we arrived. 'I hope you're enjoying your honeymoon.'

Honeymoon? I look at Emma.

'Yes, we are,' she says. 'I was just explaining to Father Davide, darling, that the reason I don't have a wedding ring is that it didn't actually fit very well because you got it as a surprise for our wedding and it's at the jeweller's being resized but I'll be wearing it every day as soon as we get back to London.'

'Exactly,' I confirm politely, giving her as much side-eye as I can without Father Davide seeing. Presumably he said he could only host a married couple in the same bedroom, but even so.

'Where have you visited so far?' Father Davide asks Emma.

As I listen to her describing what presumably have been her travels around southern Italy and her plans to go on to Florence and the Cinque Terre and the Alps, I'm struck by how well-thought-out and concrete those onward plans seem, and how much sightseeing they involve. I think I need to ask Emma about that when we're alone. Hopefully they're just the product of the same fertile imagination that came up with the wedding ring story.

'And here we are.' Father Davide opens a low, narrow door with a flourish and indicates that we should go ahead of him into the room. It's whitewashed and contains two narrow, single beds on opposite walls and one small chest with two neatly folded white towels on it. 'Perhaps you would like to leave your suitcases here and I can show you where the bathroom is.'

The bathroom is a long way along the corridor and up a flight of stairs and along another corridor.

'It's almost en-suite,' he tells us, grinning broadly at his own joke.

'It's perfect; thank you so much.' Emma sounds so sincere that I'm wondering whether she genuinely means it.

Father Davide escorts us back to the bedroom and then leaves us, asking us to let them know soon whether we're planning to join them for dinner.

Emma and I stand staring at each other for a long moment.

'I can't see how we can do the communal area sleep thing,' she says eventually.

I nod.

We stare at each other some more.

Then Emma says, 'It's lovely here. We could be sleeping in the van tonight. Could be a lot worse.'

It could be. We do have a roof over our heads and – since realistically we're both going to have to stay inside this room overnight – we do have two beds.

It could be better, though.

We could, for example, be a good couple of hundred miles further north towards England by now and be staying in a nice hotel with separate en-suite bedrooms.

'I might just go and have a shower,' I say.

Emma nods vigorously. 'Good plan.'

As I get dry clothes out of my case, I realise that, now that we're going to be on the road for an extra day, I'll have to buy some more underwear and socks. The hotel did all my laundry for me, but I only came with four days' worth of clothes and I'm going to have to change completely right now.

Which reminds me...

'You mentioned spending the night in Florence,' I say. I saw on Google Maps earlier that Florence is only about three hours from Rome in good traffic. 'And also you referred to the Cinque Terre and the south of France earlier.' That's a bit of a detour from the fastest route to London. 'I'd expected that we might have got further north today had it not rained? Beyond Milan, maybe into Switzerland?' If we don't do eight hours a day (or a lot more than that at Emma's driving speed) this journey is going to take a very long time.

Emma shakes her head. 'That's a really long way.'

'Only eight hours' driving?'

'I can't drive for eight hours in one day. And I've never been to Florence before. So I was planning to arrive there mid-afternoon today and do some sightseeing for the rest of the day, before leaving in the morning. Obviously that will be delayed by a day now.'

'Oh.' Oh fuck. It's sounding like the plans she told Father Davide about are actual ones. 'And what's your plan after that?'

'I was thinking the Cinque Terre next.'

'Okay. Great.' I'm not an Italian geography expert but I'm pretty sure that the Cinque Terre are tourist-magnet pretty villages in the north-west corner of Italy and not on a direct line from here to London. 'And then...?'

'I was thinking the Alps and a night in Chamonix, and then two or three nights travelling up France to Paris, some sightseeing there, and then home on the ferry.'

'Oh. That sounds...' That sounds like a very, very long time on the road in the company of someone I do not want to be with, but to whom I can only be grateful. 'It sounds great.' I look at her looking at me with her eyebrows raised, waiting for me to say more and... God. What a farce. 'So I'll go and have my shower, then.'

There is no shower. It's a bath, with no shower attachment of any kind. Unless Emma's changed a *lot*, she will not appreciate that.

I take my time because I could do with some space from Emma to sort through my thoughts. Unbelievably, because it feels like a lot has happened today, it's still only twelve thirty, as in there's the whole of the rest of today to get through.

If the rain doesn't let up, we're both going to be stuck inside all day. I cannot spend the whole time with her, obviously. I'll find somewhere separate to sit and do some work. I will also recheck my alternative travel options.

Back in the room, I find a note from Emma:

Gone for a walk. See you later.

Weirdly, because I *should* just be pleased that she isn't here, I'm immediately annoyed, because now I'm going to worry about her. How have her family and friends coped with the terrifying thought that someone who's gung-ho (stupid) enough to drive without windscreen wipers has been on this big journey alone? *Anything* could happen to someone travelling solo.

I decide to go for a walk myself. I need some lunch and I'd like to check that she's alright. I mean, of course she is, but just in case.

And once I know that Emma *is* okay, I'm definitely going to spend the afternoon working.

I don't have too much time to fume because I find her sitting with a Kindle on a stone bench in a corner of the cloister.

'Hey.' She looks up just as I approach even though my shoes have echoed on the stone as I walk and she must already have known I was here, and I get the strong sense that she would happily have ignored me if she could have got away with it. And that's obviously a good thing, because I don't want to engage either.

'Hey.' I realise that I'm an idiot because now that I know she hasn't gone off on any kind of lunatic expedition by herself, I have no need to talk to her. I'm also an idiot because I want to provide an excuse for looking like I've followed her here. 'Just on my way to find some lunch.'

'That's where I was going but the rain seems to be getting even heavier, and also we're in the middle of nowhere and I think it would be quite a long way to anywhere that sells food.'

I nod and find myself sitting down next to her, before immediately regretting it. I've placed us in a conversation-having situation.

'You know what I might do.' I stand up again. 'Go and ask if they might have a little bit of food they could spare for lunch.'

'Good idea. Thank you.' Emma's half-smile has the ridiculous effect of making me want to see one of her full smiles. Her face is – always was, still is – beautiful in a very classic way, which is lovely to look at, but which is not what got me the first time we met. What got me was her smile, her real one, when she's properly amused or happy. It's wide, it's cheeky, and it has this hint of naughtiness, and when she laughs you can't help laughing too.

I say that; I imagine I *could* help laughing now if she laughed, because this day has not amused me so far.

'Okay. I'll report back in a minute.' I turn round and Father Davide's standing right behind me.

'I should have offered you some lunch,' he says. 'Would you like to join us for some soup and bread?'

Emma and I say simultaneously that that would be wonderful. Clearly, it's our best option.

A few minutes later, we're seated in a hall at a long, oak refectory table with several monks and other guests of the monastery.

Introductions are performed and Emma and I are described as newly-weds on our honeymoon.

As one of the monks ladles steaming minestrone into bowls for us, Carla, one of the two American women sitting opposite us says, 'Oh, I adore love stories. How did you two meet?'

Emma and I glance at each other at exactly the same moment and then away.

I'm still floundering, my mind fixed on when we *actually* first met, and how – as a previously commitment-phobic twenty-one-year-old – I looked at Emma and thought, *that's the girl I'm going to marry*, when Emma speaks.

'We were walking our dogs in the same park in London and the dogs started playing together and we started chatting and one thing led to another.'

Well. I have never owned a dog. Emma clearly doesn't have a dog with her on this trip but maybe she has one at home. Maybe she met a different boyfriend while dog walking. I have to say that I don't really like the idea of her putting my head onto a different boyfriend-meet.

'That is *gorgeous*,' Carla tells us. 'What kind of dogs do you have?'

'Cockapoos,' Emma says, not looking at me.

'Both of them?' Carla queries.

Emma nods. 'Yes. That's probably why they got on so well initially.'

'They must be so pleased to be living together now,' Carla says. '*Cute.*'

'Yes, *really* cute,' Emma says.

Yeah, not that cute if she and her actual partner or ex both have cockapoos.

'What are their names?' asks Laura, Carla's friend.

'Um, Pasta and Bread.' Ha, okay; Emma has clearly invented the dogs and has taken naming inspiration from the table in front of us. Ridiculously, that makes me want to smile.

'Pasta and Bread?' Laura echoes.

'We like our carbs,' I contribute.

'And so do the dogs. Pasta and Bread,' Emma says.

'That's a *huge* coincidence,' Carla points out. 'That they were called Pasta and Bread before you met.'

'Well, *that*,' says Emma, not missing a beat, 'is what got us talking properly. When we discovered that we had such similar taste in dog names.'

I nod soulfully. 'Meant to be,' I offer.

'Exactly,' Emma agrees.

'So cute,' Carla says. 'When did you first know that you were in love?'

What? For God's sake. No one asks questions like that.

'It was one day when he thought he'd lost Pasta. It was the way he was shouting Pasta, *Pasta*, *Paaaaastaaa*,' Emma tells us all. 'There was something very endearing about it. The way he cared so much.'

'I do care,' I say. 'Anyway, who would like more bread?'

'Or Bread.' Carla laughs uproariously at her own (remarkably poor) joke and then wags her finger at me. 'You aren't getting off that easily. When did you first realise that you were in love with Emma?'

Completely lacking in inspiration, I tell her the truth. 'The first time I saw her smile.'

And then, because having said that, I really cannot look at Emma for a while, I stand up and ask where the nearest bathroom is, and take myself off for a fake toilet break.

By the time we get back, Carla and Laura are describing their recent stay in Sicily and Emma's doing an excellent impression of hanging on their every word. She might even be *genuinely* interested in their descriptions of each meal they've had for the past week, from the way she's tilting her head to one side and nodding.

When they finish describing their meals, she bombards them with questions about every other imaginable facet of their holiday until we finish eating, at which point Emma says, 'What a wonderful vacation,' before turning to the monks. 'Thank you so much; that was delicious.'

Then she stands up, so I do too, in my capacity as her new, devoted, dog-owning husband.

'Thank you. Wonderful soup,' I agree, and then we walk out together.

I can't help dipping my head to say, 'Dog walking?' into her ear as we go. 'Pasta and Bread?'

'I know,' she says cheerfully. 'I can't believe my own genius.'

The second we've left the hall, she says, 'So I was thinking I would read this afternoon if the rain doesn't let up.'

'Perfect.' I'm pleased that she seems as reluctant to spend the next few hours with me as I am to spend them with her. Very pleased. I am not going to worry about what she might get up to if the rain stops. I'm sure she'll be fine. She's an adult. She can look after herself. 'I have work to do.'

'Great, then. See you later.' And off she goes back to the corner of the cloister bench that she was on before.

As I walk back to the room to get my laptop, I get a text from Emma:

> I'm thinking we should meet in the room to go to dinner together?

> Good idea.

The first thing I do when I get back to the room is email Janet about alternative travel options before starting some googling of my own.

It feels as though we've been on the road on a fairly arduous journey for many hours. In reality, though, we aren't that far out of Rome and only half a day has passed since we first saw each other this morning, and therefore my travel options are extremely similar to how they were first thing: there are still no alternatives to the camper van other than walking and hitchhiking. And, according to Janet, in many European counties, including Italy, hitchhiking is illegal on roads where pedestrians are banned (like motorways), and in Italy it is also illegal to hitchhike at motorway service areas. And I don't fancy doing anything remotely illegal, because I like being a lawyer.

So until tomorrow, at least, when we will hopefully reach Florence, if not further, I think I'm going to have to gratefully accept my ride with Emma.

* * *

By early evening, I've accomplished some actual work. I've also called Thea for a chat, which always makes me feel better, and I feel that I've pretty much come to terms with the weirdness of seeing Emma again.

Obviously this evening we'll have to eat dinner together, but once we've left here, I doubt I'll have to talk to her as much; for the remaining time we're on the road, we can listen to music in the van. All good. Totally fine.

And when Emma rattles the door handle a lot before coming into the room, I am *fine*.

I'm still fine when she says, 'I thought it would be weird for a wife to knock on the door of the room she's sharing with her husband; hope that was okay,' and I nod and say of course it's fine, which of course it is, and then she follows up with: 'Have you seen the gorgeous blue, blue, cloud-free sky outside?'

'As in, the rain's finally let up?'

I hadn't seen; I've been engrossed in reviewing a contract for the last hour.

'Yes, exactly.'

'Oh my God, so we could… go?' I do of course feel grateful to the monks for taking us in. But I also really just want to get home and I don't want to share this room with Emma, for so many reasons. 'I mean, obviously I'll still pay the monks. And for dinner, too. We can find a garage on the way or in Florence to fix the wipers.'

'Yes. Although...' She looks at her watch. 'It's getting late.'

'It's only seven p.m.?'

'What time does it get dark, though?'

'Oh, okay. Sorry; I hadn't thought that you might not like driving in the dark.'

I suppose night-time driving is the same kind of thing as driving anywhere near the speed limit on the motorway, so it makes sense that she might not like it. And I cannot complain, I remind myself; I am lucky to have this lift.

'Well, no, it's...' And then her eyes shift away from mine. And she says, 'Yep.'

I feel my eyes narrow as I watch her. She was definitely going to say something else.

'Emma?'

'Mmm?' She isn't looking at me at all now; she's busying herself pointlessly neatening her already perfectly neatly placed Kindle and sunglasses on the little table between the beds.

'Do the lights on the van not work?'

She sits up straight on her bed and looks me right in the eye. 'Most of them do work.'

'But some don't?'

'Just the back ones. As of literally yesterday.'

I stare at her as I feel a wave of real fury wash over me.

I make a huge effort and say, very conversationally, rather than *yelling*, 'You know you're an idiot?'

'Oh, please.'

'What do you mean *oh, please*.' I'm veering more towards the yell than the conversational now. 'Broken windscreen wipers, back lights not working. That's *dangerous*.'

'It's only dangerous if you drive in the rain or the dark. I never *have* to drive in the dark, like I'm not going to do now.' She smiles at me as though her words are *entirely* logical and acceptable. I'm sure they aren't, but in the moment I can't work out why not.

'The rain, though?' I say. That's definitely dangerous.

'I didn't know it was going to rain and in my defence it's rare for the weather forecast to be that extremely wrong and as soon as it did start to rain I stopped driving.'

'We were very lucky that there was an exit so soon.'

'We're fine, though?' She shrugs, with a palms-up hand gesture.

'I mean, you might well not have been. We have no way of knowing what *might* have happened. God. What *else* have you been doing while you're away?'

My mind's boggling at how much danger she could have been putting herself in if she's this... I mean, the word is reckless.

'You sound like Samira,' she grumbles.

Samira. I haven't thought of her in a while. I'm transported straight back to the last time I saw her, me and several others – people I'd just met, I think – standing on the bar in a pub in Mile End doing shots shortly before getting kicked out by the landlord. Then Emma talked him into not calling the police and she shoved me into a cab, where I think I started singing, and she talked the driver into agreeing to take us home, despite my very obvious extreme drunkenness.

Weirdly, the look on Emma's face now is not dissimilar to the one she wore then: a mix of defiance and disappointment. Disappointment in *me*. I brush away the thought that, if she wants a travel companion who's willing to do *anything*, knowing the old me she might have imagined that I would be ideal. I am no longer the old me, and the new me is certainly not that reckless.

'So we—' I realise that I'm not leaving her until she has the van properly sorted at a garage '—need to get the wipers *and* the lights sorted before we go anywhere.'

'*Obviously* I was going to. I was planning to go in France – the south of France, as soon as I crossed the border – because as I told you I speak French and I do not speak Italian, but now I'm obviously going to get the wipers done tomorrow morning and I will obviously get the lights done at the same time.'

Unlike when we were young, it will make no difference to the rest of my life if I piss her off, so I say, 'You really need to be more careful.'

'Well, luckily,' she says, a little snippily, 'at the moment I seem to have you here to ensure that.'

'That *is* lucky,' I agree. Not for me, though. This whole situation is one of the least lucky things that's happened for a long time. At this rate, I'm going to be so worried about Emma that I'm going to end up sticking with her for the whole of the rest of the journey, however long it takes.

She glares at me and opens her mouth and then closes it again and then visibly takes a deep breath. 'So, dinner?'

She leaves the room and sets off at a very good pace along the corridor, before slowing down and waiting for me.

'Remembered I'm your husband this evening?' I ask.

'Yup.' She isn't laughing.

I nod.

And then we walk next to each other, in uncompanionable silence, along the corridor.

6

EMMA

'Anal shit,' I mutter.

There's something really, really, *really* annoying about someone who in the past repeatedly told you how much he loved you – adored you – but did give the strong impression of wishing you weren't quite so sensible (I was always the voice of reason when he was doing *insane* things) telling you that you need to be more careful.

I mean.

I'm sure it's illegal to drive a long way without working windscreen wipers and back lights but it can't be illegal to drive for a little bit, just after it's happened, because then people whose windscreen wipers have literally *just* broken could end up with criminal records, so clearly there's a grace period.

And who's to know when the wipers actually broke?

And obviously I am not stupid enough to drive in the rain with no wipers or in the dark with no lights.

I don't like driving in the dark at all, if I'm honest, so I just don't.

And the whole travelling-around-Europe-by-myself thing? It's the twenty-first century and I have my own vehicle and I am not stupid.

It's *fine*. I have not had a single dodgy experience the whole way. Well, maybe one or two. But essentially none. Well, close to none.

'Sorry, what?' Callum says.

'I said you're an anal shit.' I enunciate very clearly this time.

'And you are a silly shit,' he replies immediately.

And there's something about the way he says it – completely seriously – that's very, very funny, and suddenly I'm not really irritated with him any more and I start to snigger.

And then I think how the whole situation could be viewed as funny.

We thought we'd be together forever. We thought we'd get married. And then... we didn't. And that hurt. I know it hurt him too, because he cried like a baby the last time we saw each other. We both did. And then we got on with our separate lives. And I am totally over him and he's clearly totally over me – I've never seen anyone act so uninterested (I park that thought because I wonder whether it's slightly offensive and I don't want to be offended because finding things funny is a *lot* easier emotionally) – and we are both living our own, separate lives.

But here we are now, about to spend a whole evening pretending to be married to each other and then sleeping in the same room before leaving in the morning still pretending to be a happily married couple before quite possibly bickering hard in the van about the wipers and lights before continuing to bicker or just not speaking for the rest of the journey before going our separate ways. (And I do know that we will go our separate ways because I don't think I can have him in my life as an acquaintance.) And being forced by chance into this ridiculous position *is* funny.

I snigger some more.

'Something amusing you?' Callum's surface tone is conversational, with an undertone of *what the fuck is wrong with you?*

'Just this. You know. The situation.'

He doesn't speak for a moment, and then he says, 'Yeah, it is ridiculous.'

I look at his profile and see that he's definitely thinking about cracking a smile. But still looking pretty serious.

And suddenly I think I'm just going to ask something, because we're going to be stuck together for a while and I feel like the words are going to burst out of me at some point so it might as well be now.

'Since when were you this... sensible?' I ask.

'Since I grew up. And also got sober.'

That gives rise to a lot more questions in my mind. I'm not sure whether I'm going to ask any of them – whether I *should* ask any of them – but I don't get the opportunity, because Callum carries straight on with a question of his own.

'Since when were you this... *not* sensible?'

'I have not changed,' I tell him. 'You just never noticed because you were rarely sober in the evenings. And I had no choice but to be the voice of reason.'

There's a pause, not a comfortable one, and then Callum says, 'Yeah. I'm sorry. Really sorry.'

And again there's a lot I could say, including that I'm not totally being straight with him. Part of the reason for this whole trip was that I've always had a nagging feeling since I was with Callum that I *was* too sensible, and maybe I could have seized the day a little more. And then when my ex, Dev, asked me to marry him and I realised that I just couldn't imagine spending my whole life with him and we then broke up, I thought back to Callum and wondered what he would have done in that precise life situation. Particularly because, during that last conversation with Dev, he told me that I was always super *careful* about life.

And then I decided to do this trip. The one that I always thought Callum and I would do together.

Also. Again. I'd really like to know why he didn't come back to me when he'd sorted himself out.

But also, I don't want to ask that question because I can't believe the answer won't hurt.

So I say, 'Don't apologise. It was what it was. I'm just pleased you seem... happy now.' Does he actually seem happy? I can't tell. He seems rich and successful, going by his clothes and the way he holds himself. He seems really quite annoyed to be with me but that's mutual, and separate from our real lives. I have no idea whether he's usually happy or not. And it's nothing to do with me, although I do of course wish him very well.

And here's the dining hall. *Thank goodness.*

'Let's go, hubby,' I say, in an attempt to lighten the atmosphere that's grown between us.

He gives me a look and replies, 'Certainly, *wifey*,' which makes me smile, before holding the door open for me.

There are more people here for dinner than there were for lunch, with two long tables being used instead of just one.

We're seated towards the end of one of the tables, with the American women, Laura and Carla, who we met earlier, plus several other guests and a couple of the monks.

'Oh, hello, again,' Laura trills before we've even sat down properly. 'How did the honeymoon couple spend their afternoon?'

As I'm imagining saying: *Mad sex all afternoon, actually, Laura*, Callum says: 'Unfortunately I had to work. Something urgent came up.'

'Oh, no!' Several people around the table echo horror at a honeymooner having to work for an afternoon.

'It's a one-off,' Callum says hurriedly. 'All dealt with and fine now.'

And then I can't help it, because I'm curious about whether or not it will make Callum squirm, and I'm fascinated to see what this new, grown-up Callum is really like, I say, looking at him out of the corner of my eye, 'Obviously he's going to spend tonight making it up to me *very* nicely.'

He doesn't squirm whatsoever. He just turns towards me, leans into me and says, as though for me but quite loudly, 'You mean... that *thing*?' And then he lowers his voice, except it's still quite audible, and says, 'That you've been *begging* me to do.'

Laura squeaks, while Carla says, 'Ooh, *naughty*.'

And I say, '*If* you're *up* to it today,' because apparently I started a fun game and I don't want to lose.

In response, Callum shifts slightly so that he's looking right into my eyes, in doting husband fashion. I square my shoulders and look right back at him, my face tilted up to his. And then somehow I forget that I started the silly game that he's still playing and I'm supposed to be playing too, because now I'm just staring – *gazing*, in fact – at the deep, deep green of his eyes, and at how thick his lashes are, and I'm remembering things. Under the intensity of his gaze – even though I know it's fake – I feel my heart start to beat faster and it's like time has stopped for a moment.

And then he does the tiniest of frowns, which is just *cute*, and does nothing to slow my now-galloping heart rate, and leans even closer, so that I can almost feel his breath on my skin. He opens his mouth to speak and half of me goes mad and thinks about kissing him and the other half wonders, with ridiculously huge anticipation, what he's going to say.

And then he speaks, his voice very, very gravelly low: 'Are we not talking about Scrabble any more?'

I recover my wits and laugh along with everyone else and the moment's passed. Except not completely, because now I can't help remembering things.

Like, literally everything he does is now reminding me of the past.

He takes bread from the basket in front of us and I find myself staring at his (objectively) gorgeous hands. They're strong and firm and oh my *God* I'm losing my mind because I can't help thinking that I'd like to feel them on me again, feel his touch one more time.

No, I would not. What is wrong with me?

And then he takes a sip of red wine from his goblet and I can't help being hyper-focused on everything he does and everything relating to him, and first I think that the goblet is just beautiful – it's old-looking and made of something that might be a bit metallic, maybe pewter, and is intricately carved – and then I think how beautiful his *lips* are and think about kissing him.

And *then* he tears a piece of bread off and puts it in his mouth and chews and, I'm not joking, I just can't take my eyes off him.

He's going to notice. I really need to get a grip on myself.

No, it's okay. He's just going to think I'm an *excellent* actress. The married-couple-farce is the perfect cover.

I *am* an excellent actress, actually. That's what this is. I'm method acting.

I'm doing it really, really well.

Also, I remind myself, as I drag my gaze away from Callum and look around at our dining companions, I'm not feeling any kind of *love*, which *would* be a worry, I'm just feeling a bit of temporary lust, which has almost certainly been brought on by the bizarre situation in which we find ourselves, and from which I will recover very, very quickly.

I'm going to help myself to recover from it by talking to the people around us.

They're nearly all very sociable and very up for a chat and soon we're exchanging Italy-travel stories and giving details about where we're from and our backgrounds.

I'm usually quite free with details about my home life. I'm thirty-three, a special needs teacher, I live in London, I have no pets but I'd love to get a dog, and apart from my fake marriage this evening, I'm single, because I recently split up with my ex-boyfriend Dev, and I'm totally happy to tell those facts to people I meet and like. I'm also happy to share details on my favourite foods, drinks, books, films, plans for the weekend and holidays, all the usual superficial stuff.

This evening, though, even though that stuff *is* all superficial, I don't really want to go there if Callum can hear what I say. Something's making me just not want to tell him *anything* about my life.

So I go into interrogatory mode, mixing my questions with very specific anecdotes of my own that could actually have happened to anyone.

Callum has his own conversation with the people sitting on his other side, and it's all good.

At one point I overhear Callum very, very sweetly questioning an elderly man about the holiday he's taking with his brother following the loss of both their wives last year, then listening very closely to the man's description first of his holiday and then of his wife and the holidays they used to take together, and if I'm honest my heart melts because it seems that Callum has moulded himself into being just the person the older man needed to talk to, and his patience and kindness are *gorgeous*.

I'm in the middle of describing an evening in Slovenia that ended in an impromptu night swim across Lake Bled to the island in the middle followed by a little snooze on the island until we got kicked off by an official-looking man when the sun came up, when I realise that Callum has stopped talking to anyone else and is listening to me.

'Bonkers,' he says into my ear when I've finished, and this time it is only for me.

'You can talk,' I tell him.

'Yep. I can. I am no longer rash.'

'Do you have fun, though?' I regret the words as soon as they're out of my mouth because they sound rude and there is no reason for me to be rude to Callum (or anyone). 'Sorry, that sounded ridiculously rude. I didn't mean it in a rude way. I didn't mean it at all, in fact.'

He blinks and then says, 'No, fair play; I haven't exactly been holding back. And, yes, I do have fun.' He says it very firmly, possibly as though he's trying to convince himself.

I smile at him and he just kind of looks at me.

I'm the one whose eyes swerve away first.

I clear my throat and focus on my plate of rabbit stew and say, 'We did so well to find this monastery. This is delicious.'

Callum agrees and so does everyone else – obviously – and we have a mundane conversation about the (genuine) wonderfulness of the monks, and then the chat trundles on from there for the rest of the meal.

It takes quite a long time for dinner to end because the monks have an amazing tiramisu for us plus some home-made fruit sweets and then coffee and then they basically force a truly deadly tasting pistachio liqueur on us (are monks *supposed* to try to get people drunk?), which first tastes weird and then gets you hard in the back of the throat and then makes you feel boiling hot inside and finally leaves a weird aftertaste, so I would very much not recommend it, but it's hard to say no to such nice people.

When things do eventually wind up, I feel like we've been sitting here for hours, and I feel genuinely fond of some of our fellow guests and sad that we won't see them again. I also am not looking forward to the awkwardness of going back to the room with Callum, so when John and Manda, a lovely couple from Northern Ireland, suggest that we all go for a night walk to get a drink (there's been no more rain), it feels like a no-brainer to say yes.

'I might just...' Callum says, clearly not wanting to come.

'You can't desert your wife after leaving her all afternoon while you worked,' Manda says.

'Yep, no, absolutely.' Callum sounds like he's gritting his teeth. 'Did we want to get an early night, though? Darling?'

Does he *really* want us both to go back to the room sooner rather than later?

Maybe he does. Maybe he's so unaffected by seeing me now that he'll just hop into his bed and get a solid eight hours in straight off. I by contrast can imagine not being able to get to sleep for hours and to have a hope of nodding off I'd rather be more tired than this before I get into bed.

'We can have an early night any time, darling,' I say jollily. 'Whereas we can't have a drink with this group any time. So I'd love to go.'

'Of course.' Callum nudges my ankle under the table and I ignore him.

Well, I ignore him in that I ignore his meaning, which was clearly to say can we please actually *not* go for a walk. I struggle entirely to ignore him full stop because I can't help thinking that this is the first time we've touched all day. Which is probably not normal when you think about it. Like, if you're with a friend all day would you not at times inadvertently bump into them? Or just bump hands or arms or something? Subconsciously I must have been holding myself away from him and maybe he's been doing the same.

I address the monks. 'Thank you again.' And then I address the group who want to go for the walk. 'Shall we go?'

I feel like we might be keeping the monks up. I'm less knowledgeable than I should be, I realise, given that we've been welcomed here at a very low price (we should make an extra donation) and they've been very generous with their hospitality and time, and I really don't know what a monk's daily life entails, but I do think maybe it involves getting up during the night or very early to pray so we should really let them get on.

'Could we help do the washing up for you?' I ask. 'Please?' It just seems rude not to.

I start to gather up the dishes nearest to me and then several other people, including Callum, join in, despite the monks' protestations, and we take them to the kitchen, and then insist on doing the washing up for them, which I have to say is genuinely enjoyable and also quite quick, with the group of us doing it, because it turns out the monks don't just have one dishwasher (I'd feared they wouldn't have one at all; Father Davide laughed uproariously when I told him that), they have *three*.

Callum's on the other side of the kitchen drying hand-wash dishes while I load one of the dishwashers, so there's no chat between us in there, and that's good.

When we finish, though, it occurs to me that it might be *weird* for a newly married couple not to walk along next to each other in a group of people they'd only just met, and it must occur to Callum at the same time, because by mutual consent we move towards each other as we all head off out of the monastery, all of us armed with keys to the building's main door, provided by Brother Francisco, who I haven't had the opportunity to chat to much but who has a lovely smile.

'Where are we going?' I ask the group so that I don't have to chat to Callum.

'Are there any bars?' John asks.

'Isn't the nearest village miles away?' I say.

'No, it's just down the road,' Laura tells me. 'It's a tiny village but very well-equipped with a bar and a shop and a garage.'

'A garage?' Callum repeats. 'What kind of a garage?'

'One for fixing cars,' Laura tells him, looking at him as though his understanding is poor.

'Wow,' Callum says. Yes.

'We weren't planning to stop here,' I explain. 'But our windscreen wipers *and* back lights broke and it was raining so we couldn't drive anywhere, and we thought the nearest garage was a long way away, so that's why we're here for the night.'

'That's hilarious,' Carla guffaws. 'Well, it's all worked out for the best. We wouldn't have got to meet you if you'd carried on today.'

'So true,' Callum says, deadpan. 'Very lucky.'

* * *

The bar's closed when we get there, but John is not deterred.

'I actually have a few bottles of vodka stashed in the car,' he tells us all. 'Let me go and get them and then we can just find somewhere nice to sit and drink.'

'Mixers?' Callum asks, one eyebrow raised.

'I might have a couple of bottles of Coke as well,' John says.

'You know, I wonder whether we should go to bed,' Callum says to me. 'We have a long way to drive tomorrow.'

I look first at him and then at everyone else. And, yes, I would prefer to stay. But also, even though he's been chatting away to everyone, Callum *clearly* really doesn't want to, and maybe it's linked to the fact that – from the sounds of it – he no longer drinks a lot.

So I say, 'You're right,' and turn to the group and say, 'It's been so lovely to meet you all.'

A good ten swapped phone numbers and a lot of hugs later, we're on our way back to the monastery. And the bedroom.

'I cannot believe that there's a garage right bloody there,' Callum says as we walk along.

'Maybe it's karma,' I say. 'We were *meant* to stay in the monastery for some reason.'

Eek, what if he thinks I mean we were meant to be together in the bedroom. Awkward.

'I think you might be getting your world religions confused there,' he says, and I laugh, because I'm glad that the moment of awkwardness has passed.

For the time being, at least.

Because, as we continue our path back to the monastery, it doesn't feel too weird being in the same space as Callum, and our mutual silence feels quite companionable, from my side at least, but I know that that's because we aren't in a small, enclosed space where we both have to sleep.

Callum's the one who's holding the key to the front door. He turns it with ease and says, 'Wow, that's a seriously smooth lock. These monks know what they're doing home-maintenance wise.'

'Love a smooth lock,' I say, because I'm beginning to feel a bit anxious about the whole bedroom-sharing thing, so I want to talk but my mind's gone blank.

'I mean, who doesn't?' Callum responds.

And then we traipse round the cloister, through the door into our part of the monastery, up the stairs, along the corridor and to our room.

'Here we are,' I say brightly when we arrive.

'Yup.'

Once we're inside, Callum asks whether I'd like to use the bathroom first or second.

'I will go—' my mind's working furiously to try to determine what would be the least uncomfortable for both of us and then settle on '—first.'

Oh, no, but I really don't want to open my bag and get all my stuff ready with him in the room.

'Second, I mean,' I amend.

Oh, but maybe I'm being selfish.

'Or you go second if you like?'

'Very happy to go first.' Callum lifts his very swish Samsonite case onto his bed and unzips it while I look hard at my phone so that I don't inadvertently see inside because I don't want to be intrusive.

I continue to stare at my phone while he rummages briefly and then he stands up. 'See you in a minute,' he says, and off he goes.

I let a huge breath out when he's gone and then open my own bag. I get out my toiletries and pyjamas and then sit very upright (I don't know why) on my bed (it seems that mine is the one to the left of the door as you look in and Callum's is the one on the other side; there's no discernible difference between them so that, at least, wasn't awkward) and read my Kindle while I wait for Callum to come back.

He's back far too soon.

'Hi, that was quick,' I say very brightly, and switch my Kindle off (I don't need him to know that I'm reading a very spicy TikTok-made-me-buy-it romance, which is definitely aimed at younger women in their late teens and early twenties but which I am *loving*), place it face down on the table, stand up and leave the room without really looking at him.

I take my time in the bathroom because I feel like I need to be properly prepared for the oddness of sleeping in the same room as Callum again. The last time we slept in the same room we were in the same bed and lay with our limbs all tangled together. This time we will of course be as far from tangled as humanly possible.

Walking back along the corridor, I congratulate myself for my foresight in keeping my bra on under my pyjamas, because I don't want any jiggling to happen, and I wonder whether we'll talk at all before we put the light out. Should we say goodnight to each other? Yes, I think we should. Weird not to. Should we discuss what time we're going to set our alarms for? Honestly, there are a lot of decisions to be made.

I'm still not sure what the answers to any of my questions are when I do a little tap on the door and then another one when there's no answer. Eventually, I just go in.

The room's in darkness and Callum's breathing deeply and slowly and regularly and just audibly. All I can see of him in the very dim light coming through from corridor is the vague outline of a mound on his bed.

So there we go. Callum has gone straight to sleep. We have not had a particularly tiring day. He can't be that worn out. He must just genuinely have been relaxed enough to nod off at his normal time.

Well.

I am of course pleased for him because I wouldn't want to wish a bad night's sleep on anyone.

I am also of course pleased for myself because I was kind of dreading the weird bedroom chat, like any ex couple would.

However.

I am a teensy bit offended if I'm honest that he has so few feelings left for me that he can just go to sleep instead of lying awake thinking about the fact that I am in the same room as him, just a few feet away.

I get into my own bed and look across at the Callum mound.

If I lie right on the edge of my mattress and stretch my arm out I could almost touch him. That's how close we are.

And he's *asleep*.

Well, fine.

I will also just go straight to sleep.

The bed's very hard, though.

And Callum and I are in the same room.

What's it going to be like in the morning?

Oh my God. Morning breath. Not something I've ever really worried about. But that stew was garlicky. And I don't want Callum to think I've *developed* morning breath issues since we split up. Maybe I'll get up before him and sneak off and clean my teeth. How will I know what time he's set his alarm for, though? Why didn't I think to put any mints in my bag? Actually, what am I worrying about, anyway? It isn't like we're going to be *kissing* or anything, is it? Yep, nothing to worry about.

Why did Callum just go to sleep so easily? *Why?*

Okay. I'm going to read my Kindle and that will make me sleepy like it always does.

* * *

A long, long time later I've nearly finished my book and I have to say I'm enjoying it a *lot* less with Callum lying in the bed opposite me. There's far too much very explicit description of sex. I don't want to think about actual bodily parts when I'm in the same room as Callum. What if he wakes up and somehow sees what I'm reading?

I don't want to finish it, actually. I go to my Kindle library and look for something else.

I start a biography of the suffragette Emmeline Pankhurst that I downloaded quite a long time ago and haven't ever got round to starting, even though it sounds fascinating.

But oh my *God*, it's dull. Perfect for sending me to sleep, you would think, but no, because it turns out that there is nothing short of a serious anaesthetic that could have me nodding off right now.

I'm so tired. I'm so bored. And I'm so *still* thinking about Callum being just on the other side of the room.

I can hear him breathing. Slow and steady and deep. Bastard. *How* did he get to sleep?

I put my Kindle back on the table. I'm going to count sheep.

Doesn't work.

Nothing works.

I'm going to be awake all night.

I'm finally very sleepy and I'm definitely drifting off...

...and then Callum stirs and rolls over and, ping, I'm wide awake again.

I suddenly snap.

'I want to kill you,' I hiss.

'What?' he murmurs.

I sit bolt upright in bed. 'Are you *awake*?'

'Nope.' And then the deep, regular, slow breathing starts again and I lie back down, fully awake again, and wonder how I can get rid of him and continue my journey alone.

7

CALLUM

Despite everything, I think I'm going to laugh.

Very, very carefully, to avoid making any sound moving the sheets, I inch my wrist up so that I can see my watch.

Bloody hell. It's nearly three thirty a.m. *Three thirty*.

Part of the reason that I dragged Emma away from the group was that it just felt too odd socialising like that with her, and the other part was that I thought we should both get a good night's sleep given tomorrow's long (I hope) drive.

And here we are both having been awake the whole time.

I think Emma still thinks I'm asleep, though, so at least we don't have to talk.

I'm unbelievably bored, and very envious of Emma's Kindle. I shouldn't have pretended to be asleep. Then I could have read something too.

She heaves herself onto her other side yet again and mutters something.

I really think she just said, 'Stupid shit.'

She says it again. Yep. I'm guessing she's jealous of my supposed deep sleep during her extreme wakefulness.

I laugh. I can't help it.

'Did you just *laugh*?' she asks.

'Yep.'

'Why?'

'No reason.'

'Callum.' She's speaking quite quietly but she sounds as though she's on the brink of screaming, which unfortunately just makes me want to laugh more. 'Are. You. Awake?'

'Mmhmm?'

'How long have you been awake?' She definitely isn't finding this moment as funny as I am.

To be fair, I don't actually know why I'm finding it funny. Possibly exhaustion-induced hysteria.

I always wonder whether the perpetrators of really successful crimes are tempted to tell people about their warped cleverness. It's hard keeping secrets. And apparently I suddenly want to boast about my own cleverness.

'The whole time,' I tell her.

'Sorry, what?'

'I didn't want to disturb you or have any awkwardness so I pretended to be asleep,' I explain.

'Didn't want to disturb me?' Her voice is rising. 'But I've been awake the whole time. I'm one of the most tired women on the planet right now because I can't sleep because of you and your stupid deep sleep-breathing but you haven't even been to sleep and you've been faking it this whole time?'

'You had your Kindle, though?' I offer.

'I didn't want to read. I just wanted to sleep. What time is it?'

She scrabbles around on the table between us, as I say, 'Three thirtyish.'

'Noooo. I'm going to die of tiredness.' She scrabbles some more and then switches the bedside light on.

I blink a lot, because the bulb's aimed directly into my eyes.

When the light's image has cleared from my vision, I see that she's propped herself up on her pillows and has her arms crossed over her chest and is glaring at me.

'I just want to remind you...' I begin.

'Shut up.' She pulls one of her pillows out from behind her and throws it at me.

I catch it and say, 'That I haven't been to sleep either and I was trying to *help*.'

'Oh, yes. Fair point. Sorry.' She drops her annoyance very suddenly and smiles at me, and I have to work hard to ignore how beautiful she looks with her bed-tousled hair and the smile and her big pyjama T-shirt falling off her shoulder. I glimpse a bra strap before I whip my eyes away from anywhere near her body. I'm pretty sure that will have been some strategic bra-wearing and hope she didn't think I might in any way be tempted into trying any kind of intimacy.

I mean, she's attractive, of course she is.

I mean, *gorgeous*.

But I would never, *never* consider going back to where we were. We were so, so wrong for each other. I hurt her. I hurt myself. I'm not risking that again.

And physical attraction means absolutely nothing.

'I think...' There's a frog in my throat. I swallow and try again. 'Maybe I should sleep somewhere else.'

'But then everyone will wonder whether we have a problem in our marriage.'

'But we *do* have a problem, which is that we are not in fact married? And the monks aren't going to kick us out in the middle of the night, are they? And we're not going to stay friends with these people who we've met under false marriage pretences. So it really doesn't matter, does it?'

Emma nods slowly. 'You make a series of very valid points.'

'I know.'

'I'm going to be honest. I would *love* it if you slept somewhere else because I'm so, so tired – too tired to be polite – and I'm *never* going to get to sleep with you in the same room.'

'Likewise,' I agree.

'But what if you can't find anywhere comfortable?'

'Then I will be awake all night just like I would be awake in here but you'll be asleep so between us we'll have gained some sleep and that'll be a win? And it's more important for you to sleep because you're the one who'll be driving.'

'You're a genius and a saint,' she says. 'Thank you, thank you, thank you.'

I laugh. 'My pleasure.'

I swing my legs out of bed and shove my feet into my shoes, gather up my phone and a jumper and head for the door.

'Callum?' She's already sounding sleepy.

'Mmm?'

'Did I say thank you?'

Oh *God*, I love her smile.

'Yeah,' I say. 'You did. But if you remember, I owe you. And you're the one driving so you need the sleep.'

'Mmm.' She's slid down the bed and turned on her side and her long lashes are against her cheek. Her breathing is going rhythmic-sleepy before I even have the door fully open.

I have to battle with myself not to go over to her bed and basically tuck her in.

'Night,' I say instead. 'You should lock the door from inside.'

She just wriggles a bit in the bed, so I step outside and close the door very quietly behind me, before locking it on my side and sliding the key under the door.

I wander around, tiptoe-fashion, for a couple of minutes before finding a communal lounge area, where I settle myself in a (fairly) comfortable armchair.

It's now heading towards four a.m. and sitting in the chair free of Emma's presence I'm finally very sleepy.

* * *

I wake up to broad daylight, a cricked neck (and possibly a bit of a dribble; sleeping upright is not flattering) and one of the monks standing next to me with a concerned look on his face.

Before he has the chance to enquire about the state of my marriage or anything else, I stand up and say, 'I got locked out of the room going to the loo and didn't want to wake my wife, so I decided to wait here until she woke up, but I must have nodded off. I'll go and wake her now. Good morning.'

On my way to the room, I check my phone and see that it's now quarter past eight, so hopefully it isn't too early for Emma to wake up, despite our very late night.

Obviously, I genuinely am in fact locked out, having put my key under the door, so I knock to wake Emma. No response. I knock again. Then I phone. Then I knock really loudly. I know that logically of course she's fine but worry's clawing at the edges of my brain, so I give the door a huge hammering and accompany it with a bit of a shout.

Two other doors along the corridor open before I hear Emma's muffled voice saying, 'Yes?'

I smile at the heads poking out of the other rooms while I say, 'Would you be able to let me in?'

Emma says something that sounds like *Unphnh*, and nothing happens.

I knock again, and finally hear a thud inside and then the key rattles in the lock and the door's opened.

'Morning.' I smile.

She blinks at me, heavy-lidded, and staggers back to her bed where she burrows back under the covers.

'Time?' she asks.

'Eight fifteen.'

'Too early.' She pulls a pillow over her head.

'It *is* early,' I concede, 'if you've been up late. But also it isn't that early if you have to get washed in a not-very-up-to-date bathroom, breakfasted, packed, back to the van and over to the garage before setting off on a long journey.'

Emma mumbles something that I can't make out and I sit down on my bed.

'What?' I ask.

'You go first,' she manages to say.

Twenty minutes later I'm washed and dressed and packed and ready to go and Emma... is still looking dead to the world, buried beneath sheets and pillows.

'Obviously I don't want to be rude,' I tell her, 'but also I do think you should consider getting up sooner rather than later.'

'Nooooo,' she moans.

I remember this. When we were together I had extensive experience of Emma in the mornings, and she was not good at getting out of bed. She did, though, love her breakfasts.

'I think breakfast finishes at nine,' I lie.

'Really?' she asks through the pillow.

'Yup.'

'Fuckssake.' She sticks one foot out from under the sheets, which from memory is a very good sign.

'Are you skipping breakfast?' I ask, faux-innocent. I'm not ashamed to use a successful blackmail tool when I find one.

'No.' She stretches the foot. Then she flings an arm above the covers.

And that action is so familiar and was once so loved by me as being so very Emma, that all at once something inside me kind of breaks, and I have to swallow hard before I'm able to speak normally again.

'So I guess you should...' I prompt.

'Yes, yes, yes,' she grumbles.

And then all of a sudden she rolls over and sits up and looks at me. The intimacy of looking at her sleep-creased face and mussed hair and seeing the sleepy half-smile she directs at me nearly kills me.

'Why don't I wait outside while you get up?' I check my watch. 'I'll be back in fifteen minutes?'

'Twenty.'

I laugh. 'Deal.'

Unless the past twelve years have changed her, Emma is not going to be ready in twenty minutes' time.

Twenty-one minutes later I'm back at the room after a short stroll outside (the clear sky and daylight allowed me to see that we're in a stunningly beautiful location) and Emma is... ready. And tapping her watch when I walk into the room.

'Oh,' I say.

'You didn't think I'd be ready, did you?'

'Nope,' I admit.

'Yeah, like you, I'm not exactly the same as I was when I was young.'

I don't need to think about what sounded like an edge of bitterness to her words, because it probably isn't surprising if she feels that way towards me, and there's nothing I can do about it. We won't be seeing each other after this, anyway, so it doesn't really matter.

* * *

Emma greets those of our fellow guests who are currently at the breakfast table as though they're long-lost best friends. There's a lot of hugging, accompanied by Emma's hair narrowly missing yoghurt pots and glasses of orange juice. This is what Emma does, I remember. Half the time if I asked her how she knew a very good friend, she'd have told me she met them on a train or in the road or at a gig. I'm pretty sure she met her friend Samira sitting on adjacent tables in a pizza place and they bonded over their mutual love of parmesan rice balls.

I'm having my hand shaken hard by several of the men, and it seems like I have several new best friends too.

I'm pretty sure that the second we leave, Emma's going to want to text everyone from here and explain about the marriage lie because she *will* end up staying in touch with one or two of them long term and she will *not* want to do that under false pretences.

It's busy and there's only one table laid for breakfast, so we end up squished on a bench at the end of it. (I walked to the other end with my plate but lovely Laura wouldn't hear of newly-marrieds spending one meal seated so far from each other.)

I'm getting more used to being physically around Emma now, so I'm managing to be pretty grown-up about our thighs being pressed up against each other and the fact that I almost elbowed her in the boob when I was buttering some bread.

Really grown-up, actually.

I mean, I'm very, very conscious of her proximity. I can feel her warmth against my leg and if I turn my head in her direction I get a faceful of her hair, which smells lovely. At one point she nearly falls off the bench and I have to shoot an arm out to catch her, and am then reminded of how well she used to fit in my arms, like we were created specifically to go together, but really, I'm cool about it. Genuinely.

There's no private chat between us, because there are lots of people around and everyone's discussing their onward journey or sightseeing plans, until Emma suddenly turns to me, hitting me in the face with her hair, and says, 'A lot of people are still trickling in for breakfast.'

I nod.

'What time is it?'

'Don't know. Can't get to my phone. Maybe half past. Maybe even quarter to.'

'Hmm, did you not tell me that breakfast finishes at nine?'

'Whoops,' I say.

'You lied.' She shakes her head and tuts.

And I look at her upturned face and I can't take my eyes off her lips, which are slightly moist from the sip of juice she just took and a tiny bit pursed. A coil of hair has escaped from her ponytail, framing her face beautifully.

'Cheeky,' she says.

I nod, because I have no idea what we were talking about. All I can think about is the way her lips moved when she spoke, and the way she's now gazing at me in the same way I'm looking at her.

'I...' I begin.

And then Laura shrieks, 'You two are too cute. Just *eating each other up* with your eyes. Love it. Can I get a photo?' She's snapping before she's finished speaking and then she checks the photos she's taken and selects the best one and puts it on our 'Montecastello Monastery' group chat that she set up for us all last night.

And there we are in the photo, Emma and me, looking at each other, and it's horrifying, because we really are doing an excellent impression of a besotted couple. From my side I'm very aware that in that moment I wasn't acting, I was just... well, briefly besotted. In a lustful way I think. And Emma was either doing some fantastic acting or feeling pretty similar in that moment.

'Lovely,' Emma says in a slightly strangled voice.

'Yeah, thanks,' I say.

We look at each other and at the exact same moment give a small nod and indicate the door with our eyes.

'It's been so wonderful to meet you all,' Emma says, 'and we'd both love to stay and talk, but we have to get going. Long day ahead.'

It takes us a long time to extricate ourselves from all the genuinely lovely holidaymakers and then a further few minutes of chat with the very friendly monks before we're back on the road with our bags.

'I cannot *believe*,' Emma says as she manoeuvres her case around a muddy puddle that the sun hasn't reached because of the large tree above it, 'that we have to walk all the way back now.'

'Yeah.'

Once we're about fifty feet down the lane, Emma looks over her shoulder and swivels her head in all directions.

'Honestly,' I say. 'You might as well have put a sign with large neon letters on your head announcing that you're now planning to gossip and you don't want anyone to hear.'

'Well, duh,' she says. 'I *am* planning to gossip and I *don't* want anyone to hear.' She dives straight in. 'Did you hear what John and Manda and those two Croatian girls ended up doing last night? Half of me wishes I'd been there too and the other half is ecstatic that I wasn't.'

'I did hear and yes, me too.'

And just like that we slip straight back into the way we always used to dissect evenings out. I go with it because walking in silence is actually quite hard work, and talking about other people is way easier.

The conversation carries us all the way back to the clearing and the van.

'Hey, Miranda,' Emma says when we get to the van. As in, she is addressing the *van* as *Miranda*. 'I've missed you.'

'Sorry, what?' I say as we place (me) and throw (Emma) our cases into the back.

'I've missed her.' Emma's in the driving seat and jiggling the key in the ignition and we're back to the same routine that I now realise she probably does every time.

'I have a few questions,' I say.

'Mmm?' She's concentrating on coaxing the engine into life. It suddenly starts and she says, 'Thank goodness.'

'Yeah, thank goodness. That leads me on to my first question.' I watch her as she manoeuvres us out of the clearing and I have to say that for someone who only passed their test three months ago she's doing a good job of it; it can't be easy to drive a vehicle as old and with such a terrible turning circle as this. 'How many times has—' I cannot bring myself to say *Miranda* '—it failed completely to start?'

'None.' Emma's tone is triumphant.

I decide not to point out that there's a first time for everything. I'm really going to have to hope that we aren't heading towards another enforced stay somewhere while we get the engine fixed.

'Another question I have is, just: Miranda? Is that a new name for her – it – today? I don't think you called it that yesterday?'

'I feel like the ice between us has been broken,' she says. 'And yesterday I felt like you'd judge me for calling her Miranda.'

What, like I'm not judging her now?

'So it – she – is always called Miranda?'

'Yes.' Emma's tone turns saccharine. 'I think *all* vehicles have souls and you just have to find the right name for them. Also trees, obviously. And also wooden furniture because it comes from trees.'

I stare at her and she looks straight ahead serenely as she drives us back towards the monastery and the garage.

'That's... great,' I say eventually.

'Ha, ha, ha.' Emma cackles. 'No, I do not believe that vehicles have souls. But the previous owner was very fond of Miranda and said he would only sell her to me if I promised to continue to call her by her given name. And so I do.'

'Because you don't want to break a promise to a man who cannot see you?'

'*Miranda* can see me. And shh, she can hear, too. Stop being so rude.'

'Sorry,' I say, and she grins, and I realise that over the past twenty-four hours we've wound up in a place we've never been in before: two separate, very much not-a-couple people, who could be quite good friends. Very good friends, I think.

I don't *want* to be friends with her, though, if I'm honest; it's too weird. And also, I could easily allow myself to slip into a more-than-friends situation, because what's not to, frankly, adore about her?

Obviously, she might not feel the same way; for all I know she's looking at me the whole time going: what was I *thinking*? Even if she is, though, I'm just not going there. That would be one of the most stupid things I've ever done (and when I was younger I did a lot of stupid things). You should never go back. And we demonstrated quite comprehensively when we were young that we weren't right for each other. And what if being with her made me stupid again? I'd just hurt her, and myself, all over again.

Stupid to even think of it.

Now we've left the monastery we can easily not talk much and obviously we'll have separate rooms for however many more nights we're on the road, and, yep, it would have to be a conscious decision to go down any kind of romantic route.

Not going there.

8

EMMA

When we arrive at the garage, there's no one to be seen initially.

Callum and I both get out and look around. There's still no one to be seen.

'You have to be fecking joking,' Callum almost howls. 'We are never, ever going to get out of here.'

'So when Azim told you that I was happy to give you a lift, did he give you a time frame?' I keep meaning to ask that question and then get distracted. 'I feel like you're a lot less keen than I am to sightsee in Florence.' One of the few good things about Callum as a travel companion is that I know him very well – well, *knew* him, but I don't think people's basic personalities change that much – and I know I don't have to pussyfoot around with him. 'I'm getting the impression that you just want to get straight back to London as fast as you can. Which obviously makes sense given that if it hadn't been for the ash you'd have just got a plane yesterday.' I'm thinking out loud now.

'Well, yes, obviously I was expecting to be home yesterday.' He looks at me. 'But I refuse to cause you in any way to cut your trip short and it sounds a lot of fun—' I don't think I've ever heard him sound so fake when he's trying to be sincere '—and so I'd love to accompany you on the rest of it, if you're happy to have me. And obviously when you're passing through a major city I could of course hop out of the van if there are any other transport options.'

Another good thing about Callum is that he's always made me laugh, and now is no exception, although usually he's intending to be funny, and he definitely wasn't trying to be just now.

I can't help sniggering out loud as I say, 'I'm so excited to have such an enthusiastic companion.'

'Of course I'm enthusiastic. If the rest of the trip is even half as good as it's been so far, I'm the luckiest man alive,' he says. 'Half the night pretending to be asleep in a single bed and the other half sitting in a chair, and now a morning sitting for an unspecified length of time in an incredibly attractive garage. Fun times.'

'You enjoyed dinner. And breakfast.'

'That is actually true,' he concedes. 'And we did meet a lot of nice people. And the monks were great. And the food was pretty good.'

'Exactly. And we can have fun this morning while we're waiting.'

'Really?'

I almost go down the 'Er, isn't that quite rude; shouldn't you be expecting to enjoy my wonderful company?' route until I realise just in time that it might sound flirty and that would be excruciating.

So instead I say, 'I have a backgammon set stashed away for just these eventualities. It's come in very handy during this trip and you're going to appreciate it now.'

'Have you been playing solo backgammon or have you been meeting people along the way?'

'I frequently lure strangers back to my van and make them play backgammon.' I smile as he laughs politely. 'No, I've had a couple of friends come out to meet me. Some girlfriends and my sister came at different times and—' for some reason I've suddenly had this feeling that I should mention Dev '—my ex visited too.'

Callum nods a lot and says, 'Great,' and I feel like I've achieved exactly what my subconscious probably meant me to do when I mentioned Dev, which was – I think – to underline that I have no hesitation (although I did hesitate) in mentioning him to Callum because Callum and I are so far in the past we might as well not have happened.

Okay, now I feel sad, which is silly.

'Backgammon,' I say.

'I had no idea you played.' Callum's frowning a bit, as though it's wrong that there's something he doesn't know about me, which is utterly ridiculous because he's the one who left and didn't come back and it's been a very long time. I am an adult and there's a lot more than my backgammon skills that he doesn't know about me.

'I played a lot with my grandmother at one point,' I explain.

'Oh, how is she?'

Callum used to get on very well with her. They had a very similar sense of humour.

'We lost her three years ago.'

I shouldn't have mentioned my grandmother; I don't want to talk about her with Callum.

'Oh, no, I'm so sorry.'

'Thank you.' I could give him the details of her illness, but... I don't want to.

It was a huge thing in my life when we lost her and, now that we've touched on it, it seems very, very odd that Callum knew nothing about it. It's so strange, actually, the way two people can be so entirely in each other's lives and then just go off in their separate directions. If we'd stayed together – and we could have done, I truly believe – we wouldn't have huge things to find out about each other, and he would have been with me through that difficult time, and I would have been there for him through whatever's happened in his life.

So much must have happened in his life that I just don't know about. Starting with how he's wound up wearing lawyerly clothing and doing a lawyerly job and being in Rome on business.

It would have *killed* me if I'd known that our lives would diverge so entirely.

I don't want to think about this any more.

'I'm going to find the board,' I say.

The backgammon works like a charm because the second we have it all set up on the van's table and Callum's rolled up his sleeves and flexed his wrists and told me to prepare to lose – and *then* admitted he doesn't even know the rules – a man who looks like he might be in charge of the garage turns up.

We both stand up to rush out of the van so fast that we collide as we scramble to the door.

And it's *weird* physically bumping into Callum. Every time I've touched him over the past twenty-four hours – like when we were squished up against each other at breakfast – I've felt odd about it.

He clearly feels odd too, because he's just leapt about a mile and banged his head on the van's ceiling.

'You first,' he suggests, rubbing his head.

I nod and give myself a mental slap for being so ridiculous before climbing down the three steps to the ground and bringing out my best Italian for the garage worker.

'*Buongiorno.*'

I ask if the man speaks English and... no, he doesn't.

'It'll be fine. I did Italian GCSE,' Callum says. 'And Google Translate is our friend.'

He speaks some Italian to the man, who surprisingly does

understand. And then speaks very fast to us and we do not understand.

Fortunately, it's very easy to point and mime when it comes to broken windscreen wipers and back lights, so we do that instead, and soon we've agreed (I think) that he has the parts (thank goodness) and he'll have finished by lunchtime, and will call us when it's done, and it won't cost anywhere near as much as it would in London.

As we wander out of the garage (we've agreed that going for a walk or sitting reading in the sun would be a lot nicer than staying), Callum says, 'I'm paying, end of.'

'No, no, it's my van,' I say, horrified.

'But I really do owe you, plus I'll be getting a refund from the airline and I have to travel back somehow so it'll just be on my expenses. And I would pay anyway. Because, as I say, I owe you.'

'You don't owe me. You're already paying for half the fuel. And you didn't want to stay in a monastery and you don't want to visit Florence or do any of the rest of the trip.'

'From my side I'd *far* rather be on this trip with you than sitting working in a hotel room for a few days.' He totally fails to hide a wistful expression, which makes me laugh. Clearly right now he'd *adore* to be in a hotel room by himself for a few days rather than here with me. Although... actually... why *was* he so extremely desperate to get a lift back to London?

Who knows. Maybe he has some important in-person meetings lined up.

I decide it's nothing to do with me, and say, 'Yes, anyone would bin a luxury five-star hotel for Miranda, a monastery and several more two-star overnight stays.'

'Exactly. And therefore I am paying.'

Eventually, I give in, because Callum's very insistent and if I'm honest I hadn't totally budgeted for repairs and an extra night on the road.

If he were anyone else, I'd laugh and say that he could pay on condition that he lets me cook him a three-course dinner when we get back to London.

Since it's Callum, I just say, 'Okay, well thank you very much and in return I will kindly teach you the rules of backgammon.'

'Now?' He actually looks quite keen.

'That's a very good idea.' I put the box into my tote and off we go.

* * *

We amble around the village, commenting vaguely on the pretty stone buildings and vibrant flowers, until we come to a bench under a tree.

'Sit down?' Callum suggests, and I nod.

We set the board up again and I begin to explain the rules.

Callum catches on fast and soon we're playing a very competitive game.

It's good that we're playing, I reflect between goes, because I don't really want to have too much time to think right now.

Yesterday morning, when I saw Callum, I was just furious with fate for throwing us back together like this, and I was determined to avoid chatting to him too much. I thought we'd travel together but otherwise do our own thing. Now, though, I'm enjoying his company. A lot.

And that is bad.

So maybe, when we've finished the backgammon and picked Miranda up, I'll revert to being more distant.

Otherwise I'm going to miss him when we say goodbye at the

end of the trip, and I've missed Callum once and it was horrible. I don't want to do it again.

We just keep on playing backgammon until Antonio, the garage man, calls.

It's nice. It's friendly. It's fun.

I suddenly realise as we stand up to go back that I don't even know for certain whether Callum's single.

I feel like he must be because if he weren't it would be *too* odd for him to agree to go in the van with me. And I feel like there have been *moments* between us. But I don't know.

'Do you play poker?' Callum asks me. 'I always thought you'd be good at it.'

'Never played.'

'I'll have to teach you the rules if we have any more enforced stops. I think there's a one-on-one version you can play called heads-up.'

It's *so strange* how we know the bones of each other so well but absolutely nothing about each other's actual lives now.

I don't want to know about Callum's life. I don't want to find out. It would be too much.

Actually, I do want to know.

I'm just going to allow myself one tiny little question.

'Do you play a lot?'

'I had a flatmate a few years ago who was amazing at it. As in he used to compete and win actual sums of money. He got me into it.' And there it is. He's telling me stuff about his life. 'A group of us went to Oklahoma one time when he played a big tournament there, and it was truly amazing. The intensity of the competition, fortunes made.'

'Wow,' I say.

And then I realise that he hasn't told me anything about his life other than that a few years ago he had a male flatmate and he went to Oklahoma with some friends. He's keeping it light, not telling me anything more than surface-level anecdotes, exactly the same as I did last night over dinner.

It's sad. Really sad.

It's for the best.

'Tell me about Oklahoma,' I say.

He has more than enough anecdotes to ensure that there are no further awkward gaps in our conversation and no possibility of us straying into more personal details, and I find myself enjoying the walk.

When we're approaching the garage, my flip-flop gets caught on a stone and I trip and half-scream, convinced I'm going to fall over and hurt myself, but Callum's arm shoots out and he catches me round the waist. We hover, kind of suspended like that, for a moment, and then he goes all hot potato with me and removes his arm extremely speedily, and I pretend that my heart hasn't suddenly started beating as fast as he took his arm away, and after a moment he resumes the story he was telling. His voice sounds a little bit odd to start with and I can't totally concentrate on what he's saying because I'm listening to his lovely deep gravelly tone rather than his actual words, and I can't stop thinking about how his arm felt round my waist.

After far too long, I do eventually recover my wits, and then we're at the garage. The wipers and lights are working and Callum pays and all's good; Callum pumps Antonio's hand hard and I air-kiss him and then we hop up into Miranda and we're off.

'Direction Florence, then,' Callum says.

'Yep.'

'Your flip-flops.'

'Again?' I ask. 'Really? I'm *fine* driving in them.'

'Yep, you know how you tripped back there, though? When we were walking?'

I remember it extremely well because I still can't totally forget that when he had his arm round me we fitted together very well.

I'm tempted to pretend to catch my foot now and see how stressed that'll make him but decide that there's a chance it would be dangerous, so I don't.

'Callum. I have driven thousands of miles in flip-flops. I do not want to have a crash. So *if* I think it's dangerous I will change them, but I really don't. And *obviously* you would never be patronising enough to suggest that you know better than me?'

We're at a junction and I've stopped, so I turn to look at him.

He looks back at me through narrowed eyes for a long moment and then nods. 'Of course not.'

Given that he's reopened the flip-flop chat, I'm tempted to reopen the '*How* did you get so anal?' conversation, but I think it's best not to.

It feels like we're at a bit of a crossroads metaphorically as well as road-wise. We could start to get to know each other properly again, fill each other in on what's been happening in our lives, or we could... not.

We're still looking at each other, and we just sit there frozen for a long moment, staring into each other's eyes.

Maybe he's thinking exactly the same thing as I am.

My eyes are drawn lower. He's so *solid*. And big, right there next to me. I could just reach out and put my hand on his nicely muscled thigh.

I smother a laugh at the thought of what would happen if I did. I'm guessing he'd leap a mile.

'Something funny?' Callum's looking straight at me with raised eyebrows.

'I was just thinking...' And oh my *God*, I just nearly told him what I was thinking about his thigh. I am *far* too tired; I need to be careful.

This is actually what happened to me when we split up. I just wanted to talk to Callum, tell him how I was feeling about the split, because he was my best friend as well as lover and the only person who would have been able to fully understand what I was feeling and with whom I could have been fully open.

And now he's the only person who would understand how ridiculously conflicted I feel right now.

On the one hand I want to dive in and explore the life of the (still gorgeous) grown-up Callum sitting next to me, but on the other I want to find out nothing more and live this trip like we're very surface-level acquaintances, because it feels like that would be so much safer for me sanity-wise.

I don't want to have what-ifs and regrets after this trip and I don't know what I will regret more. I really don't know what I want to do.

I do know that I am not in fact going to discuss my dilemma with him.

And shit we've been sitting at this junction for... how long? I need to turn out.

'Right or left?' I ask.

'Right,' he croaks. The croaking makes me smile inside, even though it shouldn't, because it would hurt a *lot* if I thought he was entirely unaffected by seeing me.

As I work my way up through the gears, I decide that for the time being I'm going to go for mere acquaintanceship-level relations with Callum and no more. There's time to change my mind (although obviously he might not want to engage and I would totally understand if that were the case) but once I start asking questions and getting answers (if I do) I can't go back.

So I say, 'Funny how rainy it was this time yesterday and how lovely it is now.'

'Yeah,' Callum says.

And then for the next hour and a bit, we listen to music and exchange maybe fifty words, all related to directions.

I'm finding myself getting my words mixed up and forgetting what Callum just said about directions and my head's bobbing a bit. I realise that I've been in danger of nodding off. I blink really hard and do some (probably very weird) face-yoga type movements, and roll my shoulders a bit, but none of it works. I just keep feeling as though I'm on the brink of sinking into sleep. And we're in the middle lane of the motorway.

'Are you okay?' Callum's possibly been alerted to the fact that something's up by the way I'm jiggling my upper body and taking deep breaths in an attempt to shake the tiredness.

'I have to turn off.' I'm panicking a bit. 'I'm going to go to sleep at the wheel otherwise.'

'Okay, no, it's going to be fine. I'm going to watch the road as well and we're going to talk and I'm going to keep you awake, and then we're going to turn off as soon as we can. I think there are services in fifteen kilometres.'

'That's ages.' I can actually feel my whole body going into a deep slumbery state. The road is so long and straight and *boring*. 'I'd *love* a traffic jam right now.' I could stretch and roll the window down and look around and have a drink of water. Actually, water's a good idea. Cold liquid might wake me up a bit. 'Could you pass me some water?'

'Of course. And while I'm getting it, can I interest you in a joke to keep you awake?'

'I'd love a wake-me-up joke,' I say sleepily.

'What's brown and sticky?'

'Heard it before,' I say, still sleepily. 'From you.' I'm too tired to make the effort not to mention the past. 'Stick.'

'Nicely remembered. And I think you'll agree it's still a fantastic joke.'

'Yes, amazing.' I yawn.

Callum unscrews the lid of the water and passes the bottle to me as I continue to drive. I try very hard not to touch his fingers as I take it and end up nearly dropping it. He catches both my hand *and* the bottle in his (successful) attempt to save the day and prevent me from being drenched. I jerk my hand really hard in reaction and nearly knock the bottle again.

There's a short silence during which I think that at least that's woken me up a bit.

Callum then coughs slightly and says, 'So this time I'm going to tell you exactly when I'm going to give you the bottle and maybe you should put your left hand out in a kind of bottle-holding position so I can put it directly into your hand.'

'Okay.' I begin to snigger.

'When you're ready.' Callum's still sounding very serious and I start really laughing.

'I'm sorry,' I say, still laughing. 'You just sounded like a gynaecologist. Like you were talking me through an upcoming smear, trying to make me comfortable. It was very funny.'

Maybe the tiredness and stress are getting to me.

'Oh, I *see*,' Callum says, all sarky. 'Legs in stirrups, speculum at the ready and *hold the bottle*.'

'So many questions,' I tell him. 'And facts. You don't put your legs in stirrups. And I was just pointing out that your tone of voice was highly gynaecologist-pre-internal-exam-like. And question: what do you know about speculums?'

'I remember you going to your first ever smear and talking me through it in detail afterwards because you were pissed off that women have to do shit that men don't have to do, and I should at least suffer being told about it.'

'Oh yes.' I remember that too. 'Yeah.'

We both go silent for a bit, me because I'm now thinking about the past and how *young* and untouched by the shit reality of life we were; I don't know why Callum's silent.

After a bit, I say, 'So I'd love some water.' I'm not actually thirsty right now and I'm feeling a lot more wide awake after our conversation, but I think we need to conclude this.

'So if you put your hand out, I'll put the bottle in,' Callum says, and then he begins to laugh, and then I laugh too, and then he says, 'Okay, I did hear myself. I don't know a lot of gynaecologists and yet I can hear exactly what you mean. And now I can't talk about this bottle without adopting my gynae persona.'

'We can't do it,' I say, when I've stopped laughing again. 'I might crash if we spill it. I'll wait until we turn off.'

We lapse into silence once more and then I get all sleepy again.

'How far until the services?' I blink hard to try to wake myself up.

'Nine kilometres.'

'What? How can it be so long? It's *ages* since I last asked.'

'Because you're driving very, very slowly.'

'But if I drive faster I might crash because I'm so tired.'

'Then it will take a long time to get there.'

'Yes, okay, thank you, Mr Logic.' I smile at him to indicate that I'm not really being snippy. The smile turns into a huge yawn.

'Okay, we need to do something else to wake you up.'

Callum doesn't really sound like a gynaecologist any more, just like a very concerned regular man. With a very sexy voice (and that's stress and tiredness addling my brain again).

'Yes, we should talk, or play a game,' I say, hoping that I don't sound as though I was thinking about anything to do with sexiness.

'Okay. Um... I Spy?'

Yep, that's better. I Spy is very unsexy.

'Good idea,' I say. I hate that game. 'You go first.'

'Okay. I spy with my little eye something beginning with... C.'

'Car?' I'm already bored but I am actually awake.

'Yes, you're a genius.'

'That was ridiculous. Do a harder one.'

'Okay.' He looks around for a moment. 'Right. M-D-B-W-I-H.'

'What? That's ridiculous too.'

'You asked for a harder one. You have to do it. It'll keep you awake.'

I really can't think of anything so I just stare into the distance.

'Emma!' Callum's voice cuts into my sleepiness. 'You have to focus. Okay. That was too hard.'

'What was it?'

'I can't remember. I can't even remember what letters I had. It's been minutes.'

'That is *so* frustrating.'

'Yeah,' he says, 'you seemed so invested as you nearly nodded off. Okay, now I'm going to be a famous person. You have to guess who I am.'

'Okay,' I say, 'but you can't be really annoying with it. It can't be too obvious. You can't be the king or Taylor Swift, but also you can't be too niche. Like don't do a sports person or politician I've barely heard of.'

'Okay.'

'*Also*: don't do anyone I don't like. That always really annoys me.'

'How will I know whether or not you like them, though?'

'I mean, it's obvious. I like nice people and I don't like mean people. And I don't like rudeness.'

'Right.' Callum sounds a teensy bit as though he might be rolling his eyes. 'Okay. I'm ready.'

Several minutes later, I'm yelling 'Claudia Winkleman,'

triumphantly, just as we pass a sign saying the services are one kilometre away, thank *goodness*. 'That was a good one.'

'Thank you. I don't want to blow my own trumpet too much but I do have to say that I'm widely known as being a master at choosing exactly the right famous person.'

'How often do you *play* this game?'

He hesitates and then says, 'I know a lot of kids.'

Maybe it's tiredness, maybe it was inevitable all along, but I hear myself asking a personal question: 'Which kids? How old are they? How often do you play it?'

Okay, that's more than one personal question.

Callum hesitates more. For ages. And then he says, 'Girls. They range in age.'

I want to question him some more but we're turning off now and I just want to find the services and not go the wrong way, so I start speculating about which exact exit to take from the roundabout that pops up in front of us and then Callum starts talking about service stations in great detail, exactly as though he's changing the subject.

9

CALLUM

What was I *thinking*? Why would I mention children?

I don't want to go there with Emma.

While she parks, I continue a boring monologue on the best and worst service stations I have known (I am *dull* on the subject) until Emma's finished squeezing the van into a space between another van and a seven-seater car piled high with bags, bikes and people.

'Oh my *goodness*,' she says, her yawn so big I can't believe it doesn't hurt her jaw. 'I'm *so* tired.'

She closes her eyes and slides down a bit in her seat. And just like that, she nods off.

She's clearly actually asleep, not faking it like I was last night, because there's no good reason for her to pretend now.

Her head tilts sideways against the door. Her lashes are dark against her cheeks, her ponytail's coming loose and one of the straps of her dress has fallen down her shoulder a little. Her chest rises and falls gently and she stirs a little, and I just want to wrap her up in my arms and hold her.

I could watch her for hours.

Yeah, it's a little bit weird to just sit and stare at a sleeping person.

I should get out and stretch my legs. I can't, though, because we're too close to the vehicles on either side for me to be able to open any of the doors enough to squeeze out.

Okay, fine, I can catch up on my emails. Maybe I'll have my half of the packed lunch the monks very kindly insisted on providing us with. Emma can eat hers when she wakes up.

It's tricky concentrating on emails, though, it turns out, because oh my *God* it's uncomfortable sitting here. I roll my shoulders and try to stretch my back and neck. *How* did Emma go to sleep so easily? She's got the steering wheel in the way as well. I wonder how long I should let her sleep.

* * *

I wake with a start sometime later (minutes, hours, I can't immediately tell which), a little confused. I've been dreaming about Emma, which is something that still happens to me from time to time and never fails to ruin the beginning of my morning; melancholy is not a great breakfast accompaniment.

I lie – slump – there for a few moments, eyes still closed, and scour my brain for ideas on where I am. And suddenly realise that oh my God I'm *with* Emma in the camper van and that wasn't really a dream. I open my eyes and see to my horror that I'm slumped so far over in her direction that I'm practically on top of her. I jerk myself upright and she stirs from the semi-curled-up position she's been in and blinks a lot.

She lets out a big, sleepy sigh, and then says, 'Callum.' I love the sound of my name on her lips. I'm reminded of waking up next to her in the past and my traitorous body wants to do exactly what I'd have done then. And that is completely inappropriate.

I move as far left to my side as I can to put as much physical space between us as possible.

Emma blinks some more and then suddenly opens her eyes extremely wide and says, 'Callum!'

Clearly she has just remembered where we are. Maybe she was dreaming about me too. I wonder if our dreams were similar. Back when we were together, I used to wonder whether she'd be thinking about me when I was thinking about her and whether we'd meet in our dreams. I was a fanciful idiot.

'What time is it?' she asks.

Yep, best to focus on practicalities.

'No idea.' I look around for my phone, because obviously the camper van does not have a working clock. I see it on the floor, where it must have slid when I went to sleep, and pick it up. 'Two thirty. Wow. We must have been asleep for a good hour. That would explain my growling stomach.'

'Shall we get out and eat the monks' lunch and have a little walk?' Emma suggests.

'Good plan.'

The car to the right of us left at some point while we were sleeping, so we both get out on that side and wander round the corner of the restaurant building and over to where there are some picnic tables.

There's a German family at the table next to us: parents and three small children. The youngest, who's maybe two years old, is toddling around trying to catch birds.

After we've been sitting there for a minute or two, the toddler crashes straight into Emma's leg and his mother comes over to apologise.

'No, don't say sorry,' says Emma, laughing as the woman picks him up. 'He's gorgeous. I've been enjoying watching him. How old is he?'

And next thing she's in deep conversation with the woman, Danika, so I start chatting to the father. About three-quarters of an hour later we're still sitting there, sharing some slightly odd but quite moreish little cakes with them, and I'm wondering whether we're even going to make it to Florence today.

'We should probably make a move soon,' I say. 'Given that we're aiming for Florence and we'd like to do some sightseeing. Darling.'

'Ha,' Emma says. 'We don't have to pretend to be married any more.'

Oh yes. She turns to her new best friend and explains about the monastery and that I've obviously continued to call her *darling* through force of habit.

'You do seem very good together, though.' Danika waggles her eyebrows at us. 'Like a couple. Maybe the monks were fate's way of giving you a helping hand?'

'Ha, ha, ha,' I laugh.

'Yes, ha,' Emma says. 'Yes, we should actually get going now. *So* lovely to meet you.'

It's genuinely comical how fast she stands up, suddenly keen to leave.

Obviously she exchanges numbers with Danika, and then there's a lot of hugging – honestly, *insane*, how many strangers has she hugged on this trip? – and then we walk off in the direction of the van.

I don't mention the couple thing, and nor does Emma.

'Oh my God,' I suddenly say as we walk back towards the van. 'What if someone's parked on the other side again and we can't get in?'

'Nooo,' Emma breathes.

I break into a run and she follows, more slowly.

'You go,' she calls. 'I can't run in flip-flops.'

'Bloody flip-flops,' I call over my shoulder.

I stop running when I get round the corner of the services' main building and see that all's well with the parking, and wait for Emma to catch me up.

'I think I'll need to take one more break on the journey today,' she says as we get back into the van.

I nod. She clearly will. I think it's only another couple of hours' drive for someone who goes at regular motorway speed, but for Emma it's going to be at least three hours.

'I feel good now, though.' She straps herself in. 'That was an amazing power nap.'

We do make good progress and again we don't really talk, other than directions; we just listen to music. Emma starts to sing along, at first just with a gentle 'la la', progressing to belting out those of the words that she knows (not many) or just her own made-up words the rest of the time.

She continues like that and I think about how I always used to start singing the correct words very loudly and then we used to sing more and more loudly, over each other, until we were essentially shouting, and it was very immature and probably really irritated anyone who could hear us. We loved it.

And it turns out that I can't help doing that now and then Emma does her 'la, la' thing, and then I sing more loudly and then she does too and there we are.

It's fun. A lot of fun. Innocent, easy, simple fun.

We end up laughing so much that I'm scared Emma's going to crash.

'Good times,' she says, when we've calmed down. 'When we were young.'

'Yeah,' I say.

And then we don't sing along any more.

* * *

We take our next stop in a small town called Arezzo. It isn't far off the motorway and Emma's seen online that it's very picturesque. She thinks it would be nicer than a service station. She isn't wrong, if your goal is to go to see pretty things rather than get back to England as fast as possible.

We wander around, we exclaim about how truly lovely and historic it is, Emma gets very excited about how we're about to go to amazingly lovely and historic Florence, and then by mutual agreement we go to a café. (I'm hot and I've resigned myself to getting very little work done today; Emma's just thirsty.) We sit and watch the world go by and talk a lot about not much, and, okay, this isn't what I wanted to be doing today but if I'm honest I'm really enjoying myself.

As I find myself laughing just because Emma's giggling about a pigeon strutting backwards and forwards past three Italian girls like it's trying to impress them, I realise that I could happily spend the rest of the day here, doing, essentially, absolutely nothing.

I haven't done nothing for a long time. I work, I work out, I see Thea, I relax in a very structured way. That's the route I went down after I shocked myself – or maybe it was Emma who shocked me – with how out of control my life had got, and I'm happy. I have a great life, I'm entirely in control, I live well.

'We should probably go, so that we have time to look round Florence properly this evening,' Emma says. 'If you want to. *I'm* going to look round. Obviously you might not want to.' She smiles at the café owner and he immediately comes over.

God, this entire situation's stupidly awkward with both of us tiptoeing around the other in terms of having to say: 'You're welcome to do stuff but only if you want to.'

'Have you booked a hotel?' she continues, before I can speak. 'For this evening?'

I don't have a chance to reply because the café owner's chatting to her, asking her if she's on holiday, and *obviously* Emma has a lot to say and I'm drawn into the conversation and soon we're getting what does sound like very good advice on where we should visit in Florence, with a couple of genuinely funny tourist stories thrown in.

Emma insists on paying, because I paid for the garage work. I accept on condition that she allows me to buy her dinner this evening.

Oh, okay, there we are, it seems that I'm assuming that we'll spend the evening together.

And, yes, of course we are.

I don't want to leave her this evening. She's just so bloody friendly. You don't analyse stuff a lot when you're young (and often drunk), but thinking back she was always like this. She just gets talking to people. Anyone. All the time. Most of the time they're great people, because it's like she has a natural instinct for niceness, but I'm still astonished that she hasn't landed herself in trouble on this trip. And it would be ridiculous if, having come this far, something happened to her now, so I'd like to hang out with her in Florence, and stay in the same hotel. It isn't like we're going to be in each other's lives in the future, obviously, but I have a kind of 'not on my watch' feeling. Shit, I hope I'm not being patronising. I mean, I wouldn't ever say any of this out loud but I don't even want to *think* patronising things.

'There's really no need to buy me dinner,' Emma says.

'I'd like to.' It's easy to say it sincerely when it's true.

* * *

We do the singalong thing again for the journey from Arezzo to Florence, and it is of course a lot of fun.

'What hotel did you book in Florence?' I suddenly remember to ask. 'If they have a spare room, the easiest thing would obviously be for me to stay in the same place.'

'I'm not *totally* sure that you'd like it,' Emma sings in place of the words to 'Mamma Mia'.

'Because?' I ask (not singing).

'I feel like you like fancy places.' She's still singing.

'And that is because?'

Wow, I'm genuinely mildly offended. I never think of myself as thin-skinned. No one says the fancy-place thing as a compliment, though, and does Emma not *know* me?

'Well. The way you dress now.' Emma's stopped singing, obviously in response to the tone of my voice. 'You were staying at one of the most famous hotels in Rome. You just seem... expensive.'

'I...' I stop for a moment to think. I *do* have quite a fancy job, I suppose. A lot of people would find it boring (I'm a solicitor) but I do actually like it. It pays fairly well so I'm lucky enough to live in quite a nice flat. And when I go away for work I stay in nice hotels, because that's what they book for me. And when I go on holiday I suppose I do stay in nice places because I work hard and I feel like I need a break. *However*, I don't *have* to stay in fancy places. I don't always. I frown. When was the last time I *didn't* stay in a fancyish hotel on holiday? When was the last time I laughed as much as we did earlier when we were singing?

'That's just the clothes I'm wearing because I was here on a business trip,' I say. 'I'll be happy in any hotel.'

'You did love the monastery,' Emma says, maybe regretting having said the expensive thing.

'I actually genuinely did.'

'Apart from the lack of sleep and the bathroom.'

'Details,' I say. 'So what hotel are you staying in? I'll call now and see if they have a spare room. And if they don't, I'll find one nearby.'

Did it sound ridiculous that I felt that I had to make it clear that I would under no circumstances suggest sharing a room again? I think it did. I can't imagine Emma would offer. Florence is a city with plenty of rooms available, I'm sure, so there would be no need.

The hotel is a small one on the outskirts of Florence and they have two rooms spare. The woman I speak to tells me that one is their best room, with a large double bed and an en-suite, while the other is much smaller with a shared bathroom. Really hoping that Emma can't hear that I am exactly proving her point, I go for the en-suite one.

I look at her out of the corner of my eye as I end the call. Yep, she heard. She isn't hiding her smirk very well.

Then I book one of the restaurants the café owner recommended for us, overlooking one of the main squares.

When I've finished making my bookings, Emma says, speaking, not singing, 'Sorry about the expensive comment. That didn't sound very nice. And I'm sure it isn't true. I mean, you can't help where you work and where they book for you and the way you're expected to dress. Sorry. Very rude and not even right.'

'Yeah, no, don't be silly. I mean, I'm sorry about...' Well. I have a lot more than one 'expensive' comment to say sorry for, and I don't think I ever can, but I don't think either of us will ever want to go there. 'I'm sorry about the ongoing flip-flop comments.'

'If I'm honest I can slightly see where you're coming from.' She smiles at me while continuing to look ahead at the road and I'm suddenly reminded of the first time we met.

She took over from me in a summer job in a café and she smiled at me like that while our (very difficult) boss ranted at her. I think I fell in love with her at that moment. And then she resigned on the spot and we went and spent our entire day's earnings on Cornish pasties and iced tea to celebrate and the rest is history.

I am not going to fall in love with her all over again. I'm a lot older now and very much wiser.

'Ha, yes,' I say. And then making a big effort to keep things light, I say, 'So I'll look forward to when you stop wearing them.'

'Ha, in your dreams.'

We both smile.

And then we go back to the singing.

* * *

When we arrive in Florence, we go straight to the hotel and park.

We meet in the hotel reception twenty minutes after being shown to our rooms, during which time I have a fifteen-minute call with Thea, and then Emma and I begin the walk into town.

It's a lovely, leafy area, near the Boboli Gardens, and Emma's still making me laugh a lot, and, other than the fact that I never wanted to see her again and now I'm doing nothing *but* seeing her, I can't criticise the walk. It's just... nice. Very nice.

As is Florence, of course. We wander round looking at some of the many beautiful buildings and squares, before going to the restaurant that I booked for nine p.m.

When the waiter comes to take our drinks orders, I see Emma hesitate and then say, 'I'm very happy with tap water.'

'You sure you don't want a glass or two of wine?' I ask. 'I'd more than happily have some red.'

'Oh! I thought... Please don't feel...'

I look up at the waiter. 'Could we have some tap water for now and we'll probably order some wine in a minute?'

Then I turn to Emma. 'I think you might have the impression

that I don't – can't – drink any more. I wasn't an alcoholic; I wasn't addicted. I was just... stupid. I drank too much a lot of the time but I was lucky enough to be able to stop. It wasn't a physical addiction. It was just... stupidity.' And maybe a self-destruct thing because of my family situation, but I'm not going to talk about that with Emma.

Emma nods slowly. She opens her mouth, closes it again, tilts her head, blatantly thinks for a few moments and then says, 'You know you don't have to answer this question. But recently I've wondered whether you drank – did all those stupid things – because of your... home life? Your... family? I think I might have been too young to understand that at the time.'

Oh, okay, yes, Emma obviously knew about my family and she can obviously add two and two correctly.

There's a lot to unpick in what she just said. Not least that she says that she's thought recently about me. I had no idea that either of us was going to admit that we still might think about the other.

Also: yep, of course she's right.

'Yes,' I say. 'And I think I was too young to understand that myself.'

Emma nods. She looks as though she's thinking hard again. She repeats the mouth opening and closing thing, and then this time stops and doesn't say anything else, for ages.

The waiter puts a jug of water and two glasses on the table and I tell him that we still haven't chosen anything. He gives Emma a big smile. Everyone always smiles at Emma, and I don't blame them.

And then I say, 'I can, and do, drink without being drunk. I haven't been drunk since that evening.'

I immediately regret my words. *Why* would I bring that up?

That evening was the one with the ultimatum. Our last evening together.

It was the day after I passed my driving test. We'd been together for three years then. I was twenty-four; Emma was twenty-two. Back then, I would often get really drunk. We used to have a lot of fun together and with friends (or just random strangers we'd met. It was usually me who got talking to them first back then). Sometimes I was drunk; sometimes I wasn't. I was, very often, completely off my face. Always alcohol, never anything else, which was something I suppose.

At the end of the evening on the day I passed my test, I said I was going for a drive. Really drunk. In all seriousness. And I took someone else's keys (someone I hardly knew – he'd left them lying on the bar while he went to the pub toilets).

Emma got the keys off me before I got anywhere near the car and we had a big argument (even though I clearly didn't have a leg to stand on) and then the next evening I insanely proposed. I'd been intending to do it but straight after demonstrating what a dickhead you can be is not the time for it. It led to a really big conversation – not an argument because I was too stunned to reply really – the crux of which was her ultimatum. She said she needed us to take a break until I stopped being so wild. And I knew she meant it. And then she walked away from me.

So... moron that I was, I went on a big bender, with some complete strangers.

And at the end of it, I actually got into the driving seat of my car and tried to put the keys in the ignition. And then, thank God, because who knows what might have happened, the police turned up because someone had called them. I spent the night in a cell and lost my licence. The shock of losing Emma and the close shave with driving when drunk had a huge effect on me.

I just stopped getting drunk. I was incredibly lucky in that I wasn't physically addicted to alcohol. I'd just been trying to escape reality I suppose, and it had become a habit.

I stopped doing that and faced up to my life, made all the changes I needed to and basically have been a lot wiser ever since.

Apart from getting myself another driving licence. I've never been able to face doing that.

I thought I'd go back to Emma when I could prove that I'd sorted myself out but I never did. At first it was because I knew that I'd hurt her and I was scared that I'd hurt her again, as though there was maybe something about being in love that made me behave like an idiot. And then, as life happened, I *knew* that I would have hurt her by not getting back in touch, and by how life had panned out.

So that was that. Emma and I were not meant to be together long term.

And... yep, here we are.

In touch, for these few days, but certainly not revisiting the past.

There's been a very long silence.

Emma has her lips pressed together and I think her eyes are glistening.

I am an idiot.

'So I would very happily have a glass or two of red,' I say, because that's what we were talking about and I can't talk about any of what's on my mind and what I'm sure is on Emma's.

'Great.' She gives me a very, very wide and very, very forced-looking smile.

'So... would you like to choose? Or shall I choose?'

'I'm very happy for you to choose. I'm not good with wine. Shall we get a carafe? Or a bottle?' She sounds angry now, as though she's almost throwing her words at me. And that will perhaps be because I have just told her that I cleaned myself up pretty quickly, and yet I never went back to her.

'Maybe a carafe?' I say cautiously.

'Good idea.' She's still punching her words out.

I could address... things. Explain.

I take the coward's approach and open my menu.

'The food looks good,' I say.

We begin with a platter of antipasti.

In desperation, in the face of more frostiness than I have ever before experienced from Emma, I drag out some eco facts from the back of my mind about Italian farming methods.

When the waiter puts two plates of rabbit stew down on the table, I open my mouth to continue the one-sided chat, and Emma says, 'Let me guess: you have rabbit farming facts?'

'Who doesn't like a rabbit fact?'

'That's actually a really good question. You'd have to be stone-hearted not to like talking about rabbits,' Emma agrees. 'That moment when you're out for a walk or looking out of the window on a train and you suddenly realise that they're everywhere. All those little bunny tails.'

'Exactly.'

'Apparently they're tricky to look after, though.' Emma's clearly making a big effort and I hugely appreciate it.

It's as though the air between us was twisted and it gradually straightens itself out over the course of the evening as we both work to keep the conversation light until it's actually flowing quite naturally.

And then while we're eating a beautiful lemon tart and fruit, Maroon 5's 'Memories' begins to play.

We really don't need to hear the word *memories* right now.

I look at Emma, and she looks at me.

And Emma – to her enormous credit – screws up her face at me and shakes her head but then she laughs. And I laugh too. And then we *really* laugh. We're almost crying with laughter.

And in that moment I know that I will *always* love her.

That does not mean that we should ever be together again.

It doesn't mean anything. Other than that I should really not see her again after this for my own sanity.

What I do realise, and should have decided long ago, is that if Emma still has any kind of feelings at all for me, I do owe her the courtesy of *explaining*.

I'm going to do it by the end of the trip. Tomorrow, ideally.

10

EMMA

'Ouch, ouch, ouch.' My sides are properly aching and I definitely have tears in my eyes.

I haven't laughed this hard for a long time.

I think I might have been a bit hysterical.

Which would not be surprising.

Because.

Earlier this evening I was effectively told by the man who I have always believed was the love of my life that, after I said you have to sort your life out or we have to split up because I can't do this wildness any more, he immediately cleaned himself up – *immediately* – and... stayed away from me. He did not come back. He did not say thank you for the ultimatum and you were right and I love you and let's be together happily ever after. He stayed away.

That begs some questions.

Like: did he not love me as much as I loved him; did he not love me at all; did he think I was the *cause* of the wildness and that he *needed* to stay away? Did he only love me when he was drunk? Did he...

Okay, no, I'm not going there now.

I think I'll be going there later, when I'm alone.

But now would be a very bad idea because I don't want to be crying from sadness instead of laughter in *front* of him.

Callum's also calming down. He's just looking at me with a half-smile on his face. I really can't tell what's in his mind. Is he thinking about us? Or is he just thinking that that's the nicest lemon tart he's ever had and wondering whether his Italian's good enough to ask for the recipe?

I have no idea. I don't know anything about him at all. And I didn't even know him when we were together and I thought we told each other everything and were everything to each other.

I'm so far from laughing now it's like our mirth happened in a different century. I actually don't know how I've managed to suck my misery inside me during our dinner and hold off on just bawling my eyes out.

I've always imagined that perhaps he never did fully get his act together, or that he did but that he was unhappy. I thought alcoholism might have played a part in his struggles. I'm very happy for him, of course, that he was able to improve things so quickly.

But.

It hurts. Very much. That he never got in touch with me again.

Why were we laughing just now, actually? Oh yes. Memories. The most inappropriate song possible for us to have to listen to this evening.

I think it's time to go. I take my cross-body bag from the back of my chair and put it over my head.

'I'll get the bill,' Callum says.

'That's very kind,' I say very politely. 'Are you sure?'

'Of course.'

We sit there in horrible silence while the bill paying happens, and then stand – still in excruciating silence – to go.

I turn in the direction we came from. Obviously we're going to walk straight back to the hotel and I'm going to cry a lot and then…

Crap, then we're going to sit in the camper van together all the way back to England.

Maybe I'll actually just do what Callum would like and drive as far as possible each day on the fastest route, so that we get back as quickly as possible. Never having to see each other again cannot come too soon for me.

'Emma.' Callum's voice comes from just behind my head and I jump. 'You wanted to sightsee when you got to Florence. Let's walk around the centre.' He comes next to me and holds up his phone. 'I've googled. Here are the Tripadvisor top-ten sights. We could walk round and look at some of the beautiful buildings and go across the Ponte Vecchio.'

I shake my head. 'That's very kind, thank you, but I think we should probably just get back. I'm thinking you're right. We should go straight home as fast as possible. I have a long way to drive tomorrow and I need my sleep.'

'Emma, no. You can't cut short your trip because of me.'

I start walking. 'I can come to Florence another time. It's totally fine. I've been away for ages. I'm feeling kind of homesick anyway now. I actually really just want to get home.'

'Emma, obviously I don't want to tell you what you're thinking or second-guess you. And I don't want to presume to think that I just landed a difficult-to-hear bombshell on you. But if your change of plans is anything to do with me, please let me change my plans instead. I can switch hotels now. And I can happily stay in Florence until I find different transport. So you can carry on the way you were going before you gave me the lift yesterday.'

I shake my head again. 'No, I offered you a lift and I am of course happy to carry on.'

I'm not happy. I'm very unhappy.

'I don't want a lift any more, then. I'm not going to continue the journey with you.'

Oh. I feel unhappy about that too. I slow my pace while I think.

I don't want to be the person who consigns him to a week or two in Florence when he needs to get home. And, selfishly, I don't, I suddenly realise, want to say goodbye to him – probably forever – without having some kind of further proper conversation, because I feel like that's been hanging over me for the past twelve years. I also, however, do not feel strong enough – ever – to have that conversation, now that I know it will *hurt*.

I'm also not really going to enjoy my sightseeing any more, because if I'm on my own for hours on end I'm just going to be thinking about Callum the whole time.

One positive thing is that I can't really be bothered to pretend any more. I don't think I have any pride left to lose.

'I don't feel very happy now,' I conclude out loud. 'And I'm not going to feel that happy whether you stay or go. And I don't really feel like carrying on with the sightseeing aspect of the trip; I just want to go home now. So if you said you wanted to stop travelling in the van with me to be kind or polite, then please continue on with me. Obviously if you said it because you don't want to travel with me any more, then fair enough.'

There's a long pause and then Callum says, 'Emma, I'd like to explain something to you if I may.'

Oh my *God*.

I think this is *it*. The conversation. About why he didn't come back to me. Should I choose to have it.

'Explain?' I ask cautiously, while my brain whirrs.

'Yes. About… us… from my side. If I may? Could we perhaps go for a walk? Not just straight back.'

I make a split-second decision and say, 'Okay.'

I *should* let him explain. I'll regret it forever if I don't. I don't need to spend any more time wondering.

And oh my goodness, we're doing this.

My heart's racing like nobody's business now.

There's a road off to our left and we begin to wander down there. Callum begins to speak.

'First off,' he says, 'I loved you more than words can say. I loved being with you, I loved talking to you, listening to you, walking with you, making love to you. I loved everything about you. I loved that you cared so much about me and tried so hard to make me live in a less self-destructive way. There were so many little things. The way you tuck your hair behind your ear to give yourself time to think. The way you can't get out of bed in the morning but when you do you throw yourself into your day. The way you talk to everyone. Although that is also scary when you're travelling alone in Europe. Anyway. I never got a chance to tell you that like that. It all happened so fast at the end.'

'I didn't think it was the end,' I mumble, wondering if it *means* anything that somewhere in the middle of his *gorgeous* words he switched from past to present tense.

It's actually starting to feel like a huge relief that I might finally be able to tell him how I felt, because he was the only person who could ever have understood properly.

'Nor did I,' he says.

Oh.

I think I feel my heart physically crack.

We keep walking. Ahead of us there's a square with some beautiful buildings in it.

I wave my hand around. 'This is all lovely.'

I don't have anything to say about our actual conversation.

'Yep, beautiful. Anyway. If it's okay, I'd like to explain why I...' He stops and there's an annoyingly long pause.

'Why you...?' Now my cracked heart's beating very, very fast.

'Why I didn't get in touch again.'

I feel sick. I think I'm genuinely going to throw up.

It was all *so* awful. He passed his driving test. He got drunk and tried to drive someone's car. I stopped him. The next day, he proposed. He said he felt like passing his test was a sign that he was moving into the next phase of his life. I wanted so much to say yes but I couldn't imagine a lifetime of watching him do so many insane things. So I gave him my ultimatum: start drinking sensibly or split up. He promised me he'd get clean and come back to me. And then I didn't see him again for twelve years.

'I need to sit down,' I say very suddenly. We've reached the square and I make my way over to a marble statue on a stone plinth. I lower myself onto it and suck in air. We're in the shade and the plinth is cold under my legs, which helps me get my light-headedness under control.

Callum sits down next to me. 'Are you okay?'

'Yes, sorry, I'm fine.' I suddenly just want to get it over with. 'So... you?'

'Yes. The reason that I didn't get in touch is that I didn't want to hurt you.' He's speaking slowly, as though he's trying really hard to choose the right words. 'I felt that I had already hurt you a lot. I felt that you wouldn't have said what you said if you didn't care deeply and that it must have hurt a lot to say it. I also knew pretty much immediately that it was the right thing for you to say and I'm very lucky that you did say it. I should thank you for saying it. I thought I'd stop living like an idiot and tell you I'd stopped and that would be that; we'd carry on where we left off. But then I worried that you wouldn't believe me – that it would sound like empty words – so I felt that I needed to prove myself. That there had to be a period of time that I was sensible for before I got back in touch with you.'

He stops talking and I nod, because I suppose the time thing makes sense.

Then he continues, 'And during that time I began quite a lot of self-analysis. And obviously, as you know, my family were tricky.'

I nod. His parents basically never really had any time for him and his siblings and when they *did* pay them any attention it was only when they achieved highly. Callum rebelled against that and his siblings (when I knew them) were obsessed with success (and had the most amazing high-powered jobs, one in medicine and one in the City), which I always thought was as unhealthy for them as Callum's rebellion was for him.

'So then I worried that it was *me* and that I'd somehow destroyed my relationship with my parents and that I'd somehow do that with you and that if I didn't do it with alcohol and stupidity I'd do it with something else.'

I nod again. I suppose that makes sense in a confusing kind of way.

Then he says, 'So the micro timeline is that, after you made your ultimatum and walked away, I drafted and then deleted a million messages to you and then sat and thought for a bit. Thinking hurt so I went and got very drunk and at the end of the evening decided to drive myself home. Fortunately, someone called the police while I was still sitting in the driving seat trying and failing to get my keys into the ignition. My parents hired a very good lawyer, who got me off as scot-free as possible, which was to lose my licence but to have no criminal conviction. And I got interested in the legal side of things and decided I'd like to go to law school myself. So that's how I turned into a corporate lawyer. And, yeah, maybe I was influenced as well by wanting to impress my parents but that's well and truly in the past.'

He's silent for a moment while I mumble meaningless words

and then he says, 'You know my parents ended up in a very, very nasty divorce?'

'I'm sorry,' I say. I realise that I'm not at all surprised. They never really seemed to care about each other (or about their children).

'Yeah. Thanks. Honestly, it affected me way less than it would have done if I'd thought we were a happy family.' He pauses and then says, 'Okay, I just heard what I said. That sounds *so* bitter. I'm not bitter. It's just... I'm not used to saying this stuff out loud.'

'Thank you,' I say. 'For saying it out loud to me now.'

'No.' He shakes his head. 'I owe you the explanation.'

If I'm honest, I agree, and, while what he just said was genuinely interesting to hear, the big 'why did you never get back in touch' question is still unanswered.

'Are you feeling better?' he asks. 'I mean, from when you were feeling faint?'

'Yes.'

Better but *getting really irritated.* Just *tell* me what made you not ever get in touch again.

He stands up and holds his hand out to pull me up.

I put my hand into his and immediately regret it because all I can think is that we used to hold hands and he told me a few minutes ago that he really, really loved me when we were young and now... we're holding hands. I can feel the strength in his arm as he momentarily takes my weight when I stand up and now my hand is *still* in his. I'm looking up at him and I just want to drink in everything about him with my eyes. His wide chest. His square chin. The way he looks deeply into my eyes when he's about to say something important, which I think he is now. His hair's dark so the few grey ones scattered through are very obvious. I like his new more grown-up look.

His lips curve into a smile and I swallow and smile back at him. I don't think I could look away if you paid me.

And then I remember. I'm waiting for him to tell me why he never got in touch again after that last horrible conversation.

And my hand is still in his. I snatch it away.

There's a not-very-nice pause and then Callum clears his throat and says, 'Sorry.'

I point to a little road on the opposite side of the square, and say, 'That way?' in a voice that sounds very high-pitched.

'Good idea.' Callum begins to march far too fast for me in my flip-flops.

After a moment he realises that I'm struggling to keep up and slows down.

'Sorry,' he says again. 'I should continue.'

I nod as I trot somewhat pathetically along next to him. He *should* carry on; I want to hear it all now, even if I'm not going to like it.

He begins again. 'While I was waiting to see what would happen with the court case, I didn't want to contact you. I was too ashamed. And by the time it was all sorted, several months had passed, and I'd spent a lot of time thinking. I felt as though I needed concrete proof that I was doing something good with my life. I was also very busy studying and didn't feel as though I had the time to be a very attentive boyfriend. And I was scared that I'd mess up again somehow. So basically I was too cowardly. I can't really explain it in hindsight. It was fear. And the more I thought about you, the more I remembered the look on your face when you gave me the ultimatum. You just looked so sad and so hurt, because you'd asked me before, several times, to stop, and I'd said yes and then I'd just carried on. I felt as though I'd let you down then and I gradually got really scared that I'd let you down again and then hurt you again if we got back together. And I kept thinking that maybe it was me, that there was something about me that meant I just wasn't right for you, or for any serious relationship. And then, I don't know, it's hard to explain but I suppose as time went on, life happened, and the more time that elapsed the more I felt as though if we did see each other again and get back together I'd definitely hurt you, and I just... never called.'

I nod. I'm reeling inside my head, and I can't speak.

'And one day.' Callum's voice is all raspy now. 'One day, after a long time, someone asked me if I was seeing anyone and I said no, and something inside me clicked into a certainty that it had been so long since I'd seen you that we had de facto broken up, and that was that. And then I... Then I drank more than usual and I met someone else. We split up but...'

I have hot tears forming and I still can't speak.

Callum isn't talking any more either.

Eventually, he stops and turns to face me. We're standing in front of a large and beautiful church.

He reaches for my hands and I let him take them, and this time I'm so numb that his touch doesn't even really get to me.

'In summary—' his continued lawyerliness is beginning to seem very endearing somehow '—I loved you, I felt that I'd hurt you, and once I'd sorted my life out I was scared to see you again in case I hurt you again, because I thought I was a disaster waiting to happen, and then once I'd had a brief relationship with someone else it felt as though there was no going back.'

'You did hurt me,' I say. 'And it hurt so, so much that you never came back.' I swallow and then continue. 'I met... other people... too. Eventually.'

And I've never loved any of them the way I loved Callum.

And I'm scared that I never will.

And suddenly I want to be properly, fully honest.

'I can't actually describe how much you hurt me,' I say. 'And it was a killer, a complete killer, seeing you yesterday morning.'

I pull my hands away to wipe my face because apparently I have a lot of tears running down my cheeks.

'Same,' Callum replies. 'I was so pissed off I nearly turned round and walked the three miles straight back to the hotel and just hunkered down there for the foreseeable.'

I nod.

'Except by then we'd already seen each other, hadn't we,' he says.

'Yep.' I realise that it's a relief to tell him how bad it was to see him yesterday. Like I've always wanted to be able to talk to him *about* him and my feelings for him, ever since we split. I still haven't actually told Samira that I'm with Callum, despite us obviously messaging back and forth since she got worried about me being in the forest. I know that when I do tell her she'll understand, but I don't think talking to her – or anyone else – can be as good as talking to Callum. Or, equally, as utterly heartbreaking.

'I'm so sorry,' Callum says yet again. He visibly takes a deep breath and says, 'For the sake of full disclosure, I...'

I sniff hard. What? What's he going to say?

'You?' I say when the silence has gone on frustratingly long.

'It's difficult,' he says.

He looks truly tortured. I take pity on him.

'I do now kind of understand why you didn't get back in touch,' I say. 'Thank you for telling me, for being honest with me.'

'Yeah, no, I...' He's still almost wincing.

'There's something I should tell you too,' I interrupt, not wanting him to feel the full burden of guilt. 'I missed you for a long time. *So* long. And because we never split up formally, it was like we were "on a break" but not. I felt for a long time that I would be being unfaithful to you if I dated anyone else. But one day, like you, I just did.'

Callum tries to interject but I'm determined now. I want to tell him.

'And I did get engaged,' I say. 'To someone called Dev. We broke it off a few months ago and that's why I took this trip. And you were part of me taking the trip. Because when I... split up with him —' it turns out that I can't admit to Callum now that he was kind of the reason I broke up with Dev, because when he proposed I realised that I didn't love him as much as I used to love Callum '— he said I was always kind of careful with my decision-making, not very spontaneous, and that always made me think of you. I always used to feel that I was kind of holding you back from your fun in a way, that I should maybe have been less uptight in some ways. Seize the day. And that was kind of what this trip was about.'

I shiver, remembering how I'd thought about Callum then: that, even though it was probably just the first-love phenomenon, it didn't feel right to marry Dev when Callum was the person who entered my thoughts at that moment. And then after that it was Callum who I couldn't stop thinking about, not Dev.

'Oh.' Callum shakes his head. 'I know I keep saying it but I'm so sorry. You were perfect when we were together. You weren't holding me back. You didn't need to seize the day any more than you already had.' He looks at me. 'Have you enjoyed the trip though?'

He has this eager, questioning, eyebrows-raised, eyes-wide-open look, like he can't bear the answer to be no.

'Yes. I have.' The last couple of days, with him, have been kind of tricky and really not what I was expecting, obviously, but yes, I really have enjoyed it.

'Well... good, then.'

'Yeah. You know, I think this trip has made me kind of contented, happy. And seeing you has been really good too, actually.' I realise that overall I do very much mean it. 'Having this conversation has been great. I feel as though I've finally got closure. Thank you. It was very kind of you to tell me that.'

'Well, no, I...'

'Honestly, there's no need to say anything else.' I smile at him and he presses his lips together for a second and then smiles back. 'Thank you again.'

'Really, *really* stop thanking me,' he says.

'Okay.' I feel suddenly kind of giddy, like I've just heard some very exciting and happy news. I feel just *lighter*. 'Shall we go and see the Ponte Vecchio?'

Callum hesitates and then smiles again. 'Good idea. I think we continue down this road and then right.'

As we walk, I say, 'Obviously I totally understand if you don't want to continue in the van with me, and maybe you'll be able to get a train or a coach or something from Florence—' there's no sign of flights being back on any time soon according to the news '—but if you would like to continue you're very welcome to come with me. And I can easily go straight back to London so it doesn't take you too long.'

And then we won't see each other again, I imagine, but right now I'd be happy to have him along.

'I'd love to continue with you but please, please don't change your plans,' he says. 'I can't believe I'm saying this but I'd be very happy to amble across France with you.'

'You're saying I *amble* when I drive?'

'I mean, yes? It's like we're going up the motorway on a very slow-moving and not *hugely* comfortable sofa?'

'Rude,' I gasp, and elbow him hard in his side.

He laughs. 'You know what, I'm genuinely fond of Miranda now. And, yes, I really would love to continue in the van if that's alright.'

'Great,' I say. And I mean it.

11

CALLUM

Emma looks up at me, a smile tugging at her lips, and I put my arm around her shoulders to pull her in for a brief hug; it feels as though we need to mark the moment somehow, and a hug seems natural.

At first it's just a quick, friendly, 'wow we had a big conversation that was long overdue' type hug. I think.

Then I can't help myself tightening my arms around her because it feels so good to be holding her again and it feels as though some mutual comfort's in order, and then she tightens her arms round me too, and then we just stand there, clinging to each other, for who knows how long. I know that there's more to say but at the moment I don't have the words. Or maybe I'm just too cowardly.

Emma's the first one to move slightly, and when she does I immediately loosen my arms, and then we kind of back away from each other.

We're standing facing each other now, smiling somewhat foolishly.

When I see that Emma's eyes are moist again, I reach my hands straight back out to her. I always hated seeing her sad, and I still hate it.

'Hey.' I'm not at my most articulate right now.

Emma sniffs as I take her hands in mine, trying not to notice how much I like the feel of them there, as though they belong. She shakes her head.

'Happy tears,' she says. 'Or maybe not happy, but not miserable. Maybe just emotional. That talk was a good thing to do.' She sniffs again and then, as I'm wondering whether I should say more, she says, 'Come on. Let's go and be tourists. I really want to see the Ponte Vecchio.'

'Let's go,' I agree, ignoring the voice in my head telling me that I should have told Emma everything immediately. In my defence, I did keep trying, and she kept stopping me. No, being honest, that's a rubbish defence. She clearly did not suspect what I had to say; she just thought I was going to apologise some more and wanted to stop me doing that.

Oh God.

Okay. I do have to tell her, well, I think I do, but I think it would be better to wait until tomorrow. Or perhaps just as we arrive back in London. I don't know. Maybe I shouldn't in fact tell her at all. Maybe the way she kept interrupting was fate intervening, telling me that since we won't be staying in touch she really doesn't have to know.

There's certainly no point spoiling this walk.

'Oh, wow, it's lovely.'

Emma is – unsurprisingly – captivated by the bridge and its quaint higgledy-piggledy buildings.

I'm captivated by her. I love watching the different emotions play across her face; I love the way that when she smiles the world (especially me) smiles with her; I love… her. I love her.

I wish I could turn back time. I wish I could be a different person. We can't get back together, though. I think I'd just hurt her again. And then we'd split up and it would be even worse than last time if that were possible, and it would take a very long time to recover. I hate the thought of Emma being hurt, and I don't want to get hurt either.

This walk, though, this evening, this *journey*, I can enjoy this.

And then we'll say goodbye. And maybe I won't tell her. Maybe it would just hurt her for no upside whatsoever.

When you're young you really don't know everything. I think that both Emma and I are naturally very honest people, but age and life have taught me that sometimes, despite an inclination to get things off your chest so that you feel that you've done the right thing morally, keeping facts from someone is the kindest thing to do.

'There are some beautiful buildings to see on the other side, I think,' I say. 'What's your plan for tomorrow? Were you thinking of spending the morning here sightseeing? We could make a decision now about what to go and see?'

'I'd love to visit the Uffizi Gallery in the morning if we can get tickets. And then when we leave, we can drive to the Cinque Terre villages and have a look round and maybe go to the beach the morning after. If you're okay with all of that?'

I don't think the Cinque Terre villages can be *that* far away. Maybe a three-hour drive. If we keep stopping like this it's clearly going to at least double the length of time it takes us to get back to London.

Yesterday I'd have been very WTAF about that.

Now I'm thinking... that sounds nice. I can catch up on some work on my phone while we're driving. Or maybe I can't. And maybe it doesn't really matter that much.

Apparently I'm on an impromptu holiday.

I can't remember the last time I took one of those.

'Sounds perfect.' I grin at her and I think my heart skips a beat as she smiles back and then keeps on looking at me, her smile turning into something more... serious.

We've come to a halt at the end of the bridge. We're standing close to each other, just... looking.

I can see the rise and fall of her chest, the curve of her cheek. I know how good we were together. I want to...

I am not going to do that, even if Emma would like to.

It would be a terrible idea.

I drag my gaze away from where it can't help resting on her mouth and try to stop myself thinking about how when she moistened her lips just now I got just a glimpse of her teeth, and imagined her biting her lip. I force myself to think instead about the architecture surrounding us.

'That's a very gothic-looking building.' I point.

Emma doesn't hear me immediately; she was definitely thinking about something else.

'Building?' she echoes.

'Building,' I say, extremely firmly. 'And I read earlier that there's a legendary bronze fountain of a boar near here.'

Emma nods, still facing me. 'That is... fascinating.'

She tilts her head to one side and I find myself mirroring her action.

I have to fight very hard with myself not to take a step towards her. I can just about manage to stay where I am, but I can't move away. My legs won't go in that direction.

I search for words. 'Are you interested in Italian history?' I ask. Wow. Boring question.

She does the lip-moistening thing again. 'Very,' she says.

'Very?' I croak. We must not kiss.

'Soooo interested,' she almost purrs. Oh, God.

'Me too.' I'm still croaking.

We both take a small step closer to each other. We're almost touching now. But not.

I lift my right hand and very gently trace the shape of her cheek with my forefinger. I can't not.

Emma breathes a deep sigh and puts her hands on my chest, as I bring my other hand up to cup her face.

'Emma,' I whisper.

'Mmm,' she says.

We're looking into each other's eyes, and I have no idea what else is happening in the vicinity, because it feels as though there's nothing except us.

I can't believe that after all this time we're here like this together.

I open my mouth to say something – I don't even know what – and oh, okay, that's what's in the vicinity: there's a big crowd of English-speaking tourists and they barge into us. I realise that that's the very definition of being saved by the bell. We would be *insane* to *kiss* now.

I mean, it's going to be hard enough to get our heads round seeing each other again, definitely for me, and I'm guessing for Emma too, going by how she's reacted to our conversation. There's no point making it even harder.

And oh my God, what if she thinks that now we might get back together?

I don't want to say explicitly that we aren't going to, I really don't, because that would not be a good conversation for either of us. I just need to demonstrate it via my actions. We're old friends who've met again and been pleased to catch up with each other and when we finish our journey our paths will diverge again. And in the meantime we very clearly will not be kissing or anything else of that nature.

I manoeuvre so we're more side to side than facing each other as I say with as much of a laugh as I can muster, 'I think we're in the way of a lot of people.'

'I think we are,' says Emma, and laughs too, thank God.

'I think this is the Cattedrale dell'Immagine.' I point at the cathedral ahead of us.

'It's beautiful.' She isn't really looking at it, because she's looking up at me.

'I feel like—' I'm choosing my words carefully because I don't want to upset her, *ever*, but I also want to get away from too much intimacy, which won't help either of us afterwards '—given that we're in Florence, we might regret not actually at least looking at the buildings. You know.'

Emma laughs and says, 'You mean we should pay attention to the whole Florence-is-a-stunning-city thing,' which hugely relieves me.

'Exactly.'

'Okay, yes, let's do it. Let's sightsee. What's this building?' She points and I grab my phone to check before doing my best impression of a tour guide as I yabber on about the *piazzas* we pass through.

We wander around the city for a good hour, until Emma, yawning, says, 'I'm *really* tired and I'm going to make you very smug about your own rightness and tell you that I'm wondering what I was thinking wearing flip-flops this evening because clearly they aren't the best sightseeing footwear.'

'Back to the hotel?' My watch tells me that it's after midnight now.

Emma nods. She actually looks as though she's going to fall asleep standing up; her eyes are closing every so often and then pinging wide open.

'Want a piggyback?' I suggest, barely joking.

'Ha,' she says. 'A very tempting offer, but no thanks.'

She does, though, accept the arm that I can't help myself holding out to her. And off we go.

Our rooms are on the same floor in the hotel, at diagonally opposite ends of a rectangular landing around a staircase.

I walk her to her door, because it would be weird not to, and then say, 'You need to sleep. I can't have my driver nodding off on the motorway.'

She nods – sleepily – and then smiles up at me.

And I – because I am apparently the most stupid man ever born – lose my mind and lean down towards her.

We stay like that for a few long moments, kind of hovering in front of each other, and then, with great care (and great stupidity), I cup her face in my hands again and lean further forwards and brush her lips with mine. It's the lightest of touches and yet I immediately feel as though I'm drowning – in lust, in *love*, in something, I'm not quite sure what – and I kiss her again, a little more firmly this time.

She kisses me back and it's the most wonderful – and stupid – kiss of my life. I'm aware, even as I keep on kissing her, pushing my fingers through her hair with one hand and hugging her body into me with the other, as she threads her arms around my neck, that it's *insane*.

And then, thankfully – because I'm not sure whether I'd have summoned the strength of mind myself – she pulls back a little, and so I pull back too.

We just stare at each other. Her eyes are glazed and her mouth is slightly open, in an O shape, like she's surprised. I imagine that my eyes are glazed too.

'We should really both go to sleep,' she whispers.

'We should,' I agree, and then finally I drag some common sense from somewhere deep inside me and say, 'Goodnight,' as definitively as I can.

I take a step back and watch her as she goes into her room and closes the door, with a final just-for-me *beautiful* little smile, and then I walk around the landing to my own room, wondering whether I should just smack my head hard on the wall next to me, because *what* was that?

* * *

My luxury bedroom does have a particularly luxurious bed, which I am deeply grateful for, and – as it turns out – it was very fortunate that I had such a poor night's sleep the night before: when I wake in the morning I realise that I went to sleep a lot more easily than I would have expected given how much I had to think about.

The second I get into the shower I'm thinking again though.

I really, really can't decide whether it's for the best or not to tell Emma about Thea. And maybe Thea about Emma too. I'm beginning to think it isn't. It would probably just upset Emma and confuse Thea. And if Emma and I aren't going to see each other again, neither of them actually need to know about the other.

I fucking *kissed* Emma. Why, why, why?

Might she and I actually stay in touch? I don't think so. I don't think that would benefit either of us. I know that I couldn't bear to see her in a relationship with someone else and I shouldn't want to have a relationship with her myself so...

Yeah, I need to get out of the shower and stop thinking.

I message Emma when I'm dressed and we agree to meet in ten minutes' time in the breakfast room.

I spend those ten minutes reading emails to avoid any more of the circular thought torture.

I'm already seated for breakfast when Emma arrives.

I obviously did know that she was coming and yet my heart

does a little leap when she actually shows up, and I feel my lips spreading into a wide eager-puppy-style smile.

I stand up and we exchange 'good mornings'.

I look at Emma's feet, clad in well-worn Adidas Stan Smiths, and raise my eyebrows.

'Yes,' she says. 'Obviously I didn't want to have to wear these today because clearly I don't want to pander to your OTT don't-wear-flip-flops-while-driving thing but at the same time they *are* better for sightseeing.' She looks at my feet and does an exaggerated double take. 'You're wearing Birkenstock *flip-flops*.'

'I have good reason. I've run out of socks. Also, I'm not driving. And these are nice and sturdy and hold your foot in place much better than plastic flip-flops.'

'Hmm, would it also be anything to do with the fact that it's quite hot today?'

'Possibly,' I admit.

She grins at me. 'Hypocrite. So are we sock shopping this morning?'

I nod, not sure whether I love the idea of us clothes shopping together or am absolutely terrified; it's so domestic and *couply*.

The B&B owner interrupts my near-panic to suggest that we go and serve ourselves from the generously spread buffet table lining the opposite wall of the room.

When we sit back down again with our loaded plates, Emma says, 'I can't believe you haven't grown out of your full English obsession.' She's gone down the fruit and yoghurt plus rye bread and honey route.

'I actually never eat like this. I usually go full anal-healthy-lawyer with my food.' I pile oily, fried items onto my fork. 'I have to say, though, that I'm feeling good about this.'

'Because thirty-eight-degree blazing sun in Florence screams lardy English-style breakfast required?'

'Exactly.' I chomp. 'That is *good*.' I chomp more. 'I'm going to be burning calories sightseeing. And today feels like it's going to be an unhealthy day.'

What? What do I mean by that? Do I mean anything by that?

I'm going mad.

Emma looks into my eyes and smiles at me and then bites into an apple, her eyes still on mine. I don't know why, but I'm lost. I can't do anything except look at her.

If I were any of our fellow guests I think I'd be vomiting at the sight of us. We're behaving like the very definition of love-sick.

Breakfast is very nice. The food is good and I *love* sharing meals with Emma. When we aren't (stupidly soppily) gazing at each other, we talk: about Florence, about breakfast foods, about clothes shopping. (It turns out that I'm not terrified and am genuinely looking forward to it this morning, because: Emma.) None of it's earth-shattering; all of it shatters my heart, though. Because I *love* it, I *love* being with Emma. And after this trip, we won't be together any more.

I shouldn't have kissed her.

And I don't think I'm going to tell her about Thea because I think it would just make her miserable.

I love her. And I wish I didn't.

We can't be together and I need to be clear about that with her. I need to make it very obvious that we won't be kissing again. Not touch her, not be couply, just be friendly.

And I'm going to make the most of this time with her because it might be the last time I ever see her.

That's where I've got to with my thoughts by the end of breakfast.

* * *

'What time shall I book for the gallery?' Emma's swiping on her phone as we leave the breakfast room. 'Gallery first, then clothes shopping, then lunch, then back on the road?'

'Sounds like a plan,' I say. She could actually suggest anything and I'd think it sounded good.

We put our cases into the van after breakfast, before we set off for the Uffizi, me trying hard not to touch any part of Emma by mistake, which is made more difficult by the fact that I don't think she minds whether or not we bump hands or limbs.

God. I hope...

I really, really hope she doesn't think that perhaps we're going to get back together now.

It would be a huge mistake. You can't go back in time and, even more importantly, I haven't changed, have I? I'm still the same person who fucked up before. Why would things be different this time? Plus, there's Thea.

'Ready?' Emma fishes a big straw hat off the top shelf in her van, and places it on her head with a flourish. 'Sunstroke preventer.'

The hat immediately gets knocked off her head as the very wide brim catches on the doorway when she gets out.

I nod gravely. 'Practical.'

'Shut up.' She grins at me. God, I am *pathetic*. Every single time she smiles at me my heart lurches.

* * *

'So what's your usual art gallery policy?' Emma asks as we stroll along the Via de' Guicciardini. 'Ages absorbing one amazing picture and a few others by that artist or zip round the whole place saying "Lovely" a lot, or somewhere in between?'

'Erm.' I can't really remember the last time I went to a gallery for pure pleasure. In my defence, I do have a very busy life. 'I think... somewhere in between. *However,* if you're keen to go for History-of-Art-degree-level knowledge I'm with you. And if you'd rather sprint round for a two-second nod at every single painting, I'm also with you.'

I'd be with her anywhere.

'There's one painting I'd really like to see, *The Birth of Venus* by Botticelli. And his other works. And then I'd like to zip. How's that?'

'Well, that sounds perfect.'

And we share another very soppy grin.

What. Am. I. Doing?

* * *

We do of course have a great time. Within twenty minutes of being in there, I'm immersed in the 'I adore art' feeling that you get in those places if you're with someone whose company you enjoy and who's also enjoying it, and am genuinely feeling culturally enriched.

We spend a long time in there, and it's only when we finally leave, arguing about whether *The Birth of Venus* or Botticelli's *Primavera* is better in our opinion, that I remember that this is eating into our travel time.

And I really don't care about the time. I'm just enjoying myself.

'You're wrong,' Emma concludes our argument.

'Always,' I say, rolling my eyes but smiling. 'Wow.' We're both blinking. 'That sun is bright. And hot.'

Emma slaps her hat on her head. 'Should we go and find some department store aircon?'

She's an *excellent* shopper. Very decisive and very opinionated. I come away with slightly more clothing than I had expected to buy and it's all slightly more daring than I had expected it would be.

Crossing back over the Ponte Vecchio on our way to the restaurant Tripadvisor recommended to me for lunch (I persuaded Emma to let me take her somewhere nice on the grounds that dinner might well be at a service station), we pass a street vendor selling novelty socks.

'Oh my goodness.' Emma pulls me into the kiosk. 'I *love* these ones.' They are literally a picture of a bridge on a sock. The bridge is bright blue and the background is bright, bright pink. They are one of the most tasteless items of clothing I've ever seen. 'Let me buy them for you. You can't have too many socks. What if we get delayed again?'

'Thank you. I think you're right.' They're a complete eyesore; I already know that they're going to be my favourite socks forever more.

'Will you be wearing them to your next important work meeting?' she checks.

'Certainly.'

* * *

Lunch is of course perfect.

Driving from Florence with a stop at a service station that is definitely not the nicest I've ever visited is perfect.

Doing a whistle-stop early evening tour of a couple of the Cinque Terre villages is perfect.

Arriving at the campsite Emma's booked for the night is perfect. And that's saying a lot, because we have a static caravan each and they make the service station we stopped in for stale paninis and limp salad before using the very smelly toilets seem pretty upmarket by comparison.

And taking a moonlit stroll along the beach with Emma is… perfect.

We haven't held hands all day. We've bumped arms more than we should have done as we've walked. We've brushed fingers as we've shared food. We've nudged shoulders when sitting next to each other bantering.

I've been rubbish if I'm honest. I'm supposed to be making it very clear that nothing else is going to happen between us.

But to be fair to me it's all been quite under-the-radar-y and it could kind of pass for close friendship, plus it's *really* hard to have that conversation with someone you're going to be sitting in a van with for the next few days. And it's very, very hard to resist the temptation of enjoying these stolen moments with Emma.

And now, walking barefoot on fine sand, with the sound of waves lapping against the shore, palm trees illuminated by the moon as though they're ghost trees, everything feels other-worldly, and maybe because of that, I don't know, but somehow our hands find each other.

We link fingers, and it feels so very right.

12

EMMA

I almost want to laugh at how fairy-tale-like this whole... *scene*... is. Scene feels like the correct word.

Like... it can't be real.

Who gets to pine for quite a serious length of time for The One That Got Away and then get on with their life but always have a memory and hurt in the back of their mind, and then re-meet him and have *this*?

There's no one else here. We came to an off-the-beaten-track beach and it's literally just us and some seagulls and the whole scenery thing in the moonlight.

'Argh.' I trip as my foot plunges into a hole in the sand – probably caused by people digging on the beach during the day – and have a momentary sensation of falling until I'm rescued by Callum's strong fingers and arm.

'Okay?' he asks. His arm's gripping me round the waist from when he caught me. I don't need him to hold me up now... but it's very nice. I'm wearing a vest top above a long floaty skirt, and he's wearing a T-shirt, and the bare skin of his arm is against the bare skin of my waist; the touch is turning my insides to jelly.

'All good.' My voice comes out sounding weird. I think my vocal cords might be as busy as the rest of me going *OMG, Callum's arm is round my waist and it's staying there*. As in, we are now walking along with his arm round me, so that I'm hugged against his side.

We kissed last night and we've spent the whole day together in a very *together* kind of way, but we haven't done this.

We continue walking along for a few moments, and then I slide my arm round Callum's waist and he moves the arm that's round me up to my shoulders and there we are. We each have an arm round the other. Walking along in a joined-at-the-hip way. It's *gorgeous*.

I can't think. I'm scared to. In case it's all *too* perfect.

The beach curves round, and a building with fairy lights strung along its outside walls and pillars comes into view. We continue to walk towards it and as we get closer, we begin to hear the hum of voices punctuated by the occasional shout of laughter.

It's clearly a bar, and when we get within a few metres of it, Callum says, 'Do you fancy a drink?'

'Yes, I really do,' I breathe. I can't remember ever seeing a prettier bar. Ever.

There's a teensy possibility that I'm seeing things through rose-tinted spectacles today – I *loved* the service station that we stopped at and I checked some online reviews and most people *trash* it ratings-wise, and I thought the campsite was lovely when I was looking at it with Callum but with hindsight I'm wondering whether it was in fact a tiny bit scruffy and also smelly – but honestly this bar and its location are objectively stunning.

It's very, very busy, but in a lovely way, because everyone's just spilling out of the bar's terrace and onto the beach next to it.

Callum has a magic way with crowds and a whole sea of people part for us as we head towards the bar.

'You're like that biblical character,' I tell him when we've finally made it.

'Which one?'

'The one who parted the biblical sea. I can never get through crowds like that.'

'I mean, I am of *course* biblically amazing, but I think it might just be to do with being tall and not being averse to a bit of shoulder flexing.'

I laugh and manage not to go insanely fan-girl over him and tell him that it was actually amazing. *Everything* about him seems amazing today.

I opt for a piña colada because it's a piña colada kind of evening.

Callum goes for a cold lager.

I frown. 'Cold lager? Is that right for this bar, this beach, this evening?'

Callum stares at me. 'I'm guessing... not?'

'Exactly.' I nod approvingly.

'Okay. I don't want to ruin your evening but also I would *kill* for a nice cold beer. So I'm thinking I'll have the lager *and* something more...'

'Cocktaily?'

'Cocktaily. The exact word I was looking for.' He orders the bar special, which they've called 'Sexy on our beach', clearly aimed firmly at English-speaking tourists.

As we carry our drinks outside, I'm suddenly horrified with myself. I got *stupidly* carried away there by the whole we're-in-this-idyllic-cocktaily-location thing. This is Callum, who used to behave ridiculously on nights out. While under the influence. Which is entirely (I think) what split us up.

'Callum, I'm so sorry. I literally just nagged you into drinking when you didn't want to. I do *not* want to be one of those people who does that. I'm *not* one of those people. Please don't drink the cocktail if you don't want to.'

'Emma. It's two drinks over a whole evening and I won't finish them if I don't want to. Honestly, I know you aren't someone who nags people to drink more than they want to and I won't. Really.'

Two seconds later he takes a sip of the cocktail and says, 'Oh my God, that's *disgusting*.' He holds it out to me and I take a sip and gag slightly.

'Wow.' I'm shaking my head. 'It looks so pretty and I always like a punny name, but it's so sweet and soapy.' I gag a bit again.

'Aftertaste just hit you?' Callum asks, taking a big gulp of his lager. 'Oh, that's better.'

When I'm sure that I'm not actually going to vomit I drink some of my own cocktail.

'This one's very nice,' I tell him. 'Try some.'

He screws his face up doubtfully.

'Trust me,' I say.

'That's what people say when they're luring people to their death.'

'I just tasted it and it's really good and I have not been poisoned.'

'Fair point.' He tastes it and then shakes his head and takes another sip of lager, fast. 'No, no, no. You have *bad* taste.'

Which, for no good reason at all, because clearly it isn't at all funny, makes us both laugh. I think maybe we're intoxicated by each other's company. I am, anyway. Maybe Callum's just laughing in sympathy.

We laugh more, we talk a lot, we laugh some more, and then, after the Italian people next to us say they're going to order some of the cocktails that Callum got and I tell them they *can't* because it's *disgusting*, we get talking to them.

'Come and dance on the beach,' one of the women asks us maybe fifteen minutes later. 'You can't say no – it's my birthday.'

I look at Callum and say, 'It would be rude not to.'

'It wouldn't really?'

'Fun, though?'

He laughs. 'Okay, true.'

'What scares me is that I think you might have gone even if I hadn't been here,' he says as we follow our new friends out of the opposite side of the bar from where we arrived.

'Mmm, maybe but maybe not. I've got wiser during the course of my trip.'

'What?' Callum's hand shoots out and grasps my wrist. 'Emma? Has anything bad happened to you?'

'Noooo, not really.' I look up at Callum and my breath catches at the murderous look on his face. He looks as though he *really* cares.

'Tell me.'

'Honestly. It was fine in the end. I met some new people and went for a drink and one of the men tried it on a little too heavy-handedly and I was *fine*, but if I'm honest, only because two other women spotted what was happening and helped me. But it did kind of shake me up and when I met someone a couple of weeks later who seemed quite sleazy I got a bit spooked and decided that *lots* of people are sleazy and I've been very sensible ever since.'

'Bloody *hell*, Emma.' Callum hasn't let go of my wrist. 'I'm so glad that I'm here with you now.'

'Me too,' I say simply, because it's true. And clearly not just because of the safety thing.

We follow our new friends to where they've already made a fire on the beach, and soon we're all dancing barefoot in a big group while someone sitting on a tree stump plays a violin. The music's haunting, the flames make everything seem almost spooky, some of the people around us are starting to act a *little* oddly (one of the men for example has stripped down to a very skimpy pair of black trunks and is doing very strange, twisty and jerky dancing while a woman flicks some kind of dark liquid on his chest – I mean the liquid thing is *strange*) and if Callum weren't here I'd definitely be feeling a little bit spooked.

But he is. And I'm enjoying dancing with him. We aren't touching but we're close together and we're watching each other the whole time and the whole spookiness adds something that makes it all feel special.

Until the birthday woman says, 'Now it is time for my birthday cakes.'

The birthday cakes turn out to be of the magic mushroomy kind. The woman pulls me in one direction and a man pulls Callum in another and suddenly we're surrounded by people and I can't see Callum. I really, really, *really* don't want the 'cake' that the very over-insistent birthday girl is practically shoving down my throat.

I full-on *shriek*, 'Callum,' just as he pops up and shoulders his way through.

'Great evening, thank you so much,' he tells everyone as he grabs my hand and we walk away from the group in the direction of the bar.

'Shoes,' I remind him and we turn back round and pick them up before setting off again.

We don't speak until we're some way beyond the bar back in the direction of the campsite; we just march along at an angry kind of pace. Callum's the angry one. I'm not angry. I'm just kind of annoyed that he clearly is.

Then he suddenly stops under a palm tree and almost yells, 'And that is why you should not be travelling alone.'

Sorry, what? The hypocrisy.

'And that is the kind of thing you used to involve us in all the time when we were young.'

'And I shouldn't have done.' He's yelling at full capacity now. 'It was stupid and ridiculous and dangerous.'

'I *know that*. That is what I told you.'

'Yeah, you were wise then. Now you're stupid. *Stupid*. You've changed. In a really idiotic way.'

'No, I have not,' I holler. 'I've always been like this. How could I have coped with being with you if I hadn't been? I would have hated your utter madness, wouldn't I? Like I wouldn't have been able to cope at all with it. You just didn't notice. I just seemed boring compared to your incredibly outrageous lifestyle. And you *told* me to get out there and have experiences and *that is what I am doing*.'

'Not like this, you idiot,' he shouts back.

We just stand, me with my hands on hips, him with his arms folded across his chest, glaring at each other.

And then, as suddenly as he started shouting at me, Callum takes a pace forward and as he does so he unfolds his arms and holds them out to me. I step into them and then, equally suddenly, we're kissing.

It starts as the yelling equivalent of kissing, hard and fierce, but then it becomes something softer, still urgent and intense, but it's a less angry kind of passion now.

Callum has a hand in my hair, tugging gently at my ponytail, and I have my arms round his neck, with one of my hands in his lovely, thick hair. His other arm's round my waist holding me tight against him, and it's *wonderful*.

We kiss and kiss and at some point we end up lying down on the beach, which at pretty much any other time would annoy me from a sand-inside-clothes perspective but which right now is just *perfect*.

We're there for a long time and I think we're both in a big haze of passion and don't initially hear the voices that come out of the night until their owners' feet pass really quite close to our faces.

We both freeze and now that we aren't actually *doing* anything, I'm very, very aware that we both have our hands on quite intimate parts of the other and we're literally just there as though we're playing some kind of weird sexual musical statues.

I'm also pretty sure that we're both going to feel a bit sandy in places we might not want to.

'Um.' I'm the first one to withdraw my hands, although that isn't good either because now, owing to Callum being very large and half on top of me, I'm not sure quite what to do with them other than lie with my arms kind of splayed out to the sides.

Callum remains in sexual statue position for a couple of moments longer before clearing his throat and pulling my clothes a bit more into their usual position and then adjusting his own clothes.

He then rolls off me, sits up, pushes himself to his feet and stretches his hand down to pull me up.

He clears his throat. 'It's quite late. Shall we go back?'

'Good idea,' I say.

As we start walking, I look back and, oh my *goodness*, what were we thinking, we were basically right at the entrance to the beach. Another group of people are heading towards us. Wow, we could have been doing *all* sorts by now, very publicly.

I begin to giggle at the thought, and then Callum begins to laugh too.

The laughing's a good thing because it's a distraction from the what-was-that and what-are-we-going-to-do-when-we-get-back-to-the-caravan feelings that I'm starting to get and I imagine Callum might be too.

And somehow, during the laughing, our arms meet and our

hands find each other and the rest of the walk back is hand in hand. My head's full of half-formed what's-going-to-happen-next and what-do-I-*want*-to-happen-next thoughts, all of which I try to ignore, because this moonlit, hand-holding walk is truly lovely. I have no idea where – if anywhere – we might go from here, but at the very least, if nothing else happens, I think I will now have a kind of closure on the what-ifs and whys that I've had inside me since our non-split split twelve years ago.

As we approach the campsite entrance, I see Callum's face illuminated for a long moment by a seriously neon lamp, and I feel the most intense longing for... well a *forever*. With him. I don't want to lose him again. I know I don't know much about his life now – well, essentially nothing, I realise, when I do a quick mental catalogue of some of the topics we've touched on over the past couple of days – but I know *him*.

Obviously, beyond knowing that I want to keep on seeing him, hopefully get back together properly with him (I can't believe I just even *thought* that, it seems so huge), I have no control over what actually happens owing to the whole taking-two-to-tango thing.

I do feel, though, that I have a little bit of control over what might happen this evening, because I don't feel like Callum has *that* much willpower today when it comes to physical stuff with me. And I feel as though I'd very much like more – a lot more – to happen between us tonight. Because if we don't ultimately get properly back together, I'm going to be very upset all over again, and whatever we do or don't do tonight won't change that. In the short term I would very, very much like to – basically – have extremely rampant sex with him as much as possible for as long as possible.

So as we walk through the campsite gates, I move a little closer to him so that our hand-holding arms are completely touching, and then I rub my thumb against his. He stops walking and looks down at me. I stand on tiptoes and kiss him right on the lips.

He doesn't respond immediately and I go almost rigid from panic and slight horror – because we'll be sharing a very small space for the rest of our journey and if he rejects me now that might not feel *great* – but then he starts to return the kiss, and very quickly the intensity of it builds again.

I push away the thought that he was considering for a little too long what he should do, because this is wonderful and I just want to go with it now, without thinking, analysing, worrying – just enjoy it.

Another group of tourists seems to be heading towards us and so I begin to pull Callum towards my caravan, because it's slightly nearer than his.

We barely have the door closed before we're doing stuff that no one should ever do al fresco even in the most deserted of locations, and it's *sensational*.

13

CALLUM

I lie in bed flat on my back with my arm around Emma, who's sleeping nestled against me as she so often used to.

Her hair's spread across my chest, the weight of her limbs feels comforting rather than heavy, and I love the way it feels as though her breathing's synced with mine.

I love her. I love everything about her.

I don't want to hurt her. I don't want to get hurt either. But most of all I don't want to hurt her.

I pull her a little bit more tightly against me and stare up at the caravan's tiled ceiling.

There are stains on it. How did they get there?

I look around the caravan. Its thin grey curtains are nothing against the imprint-your-retina-strong morning sunlight, so I'm almost blinking from the brightness. The interior of the caravan is very brown. Shit-brown. And the fixtures and fittings, such as they are, are only just the right side of acceptable for a very low-price rental.

It's an incongruous place to have had the most glorious sex

with the only woman I've ever loved, who I'm going to have to say goodbye to soon.

I have to tell her about Thea. I thought I'd decided that I wasn't going to but I'm going to have to; I can't just walk away from her without giving her some kind of a good reason.

The thing is, though, that I can't leave Emma right now. I can't. Not just because when I do it's going to be a huge wrench, but because I honestly can't bear the thought of abandoning her to the situations she gets into due to her friendliness. And the way people are just drawn to her. Plus, if she feels anywhere near as heart-broken as I'm going to, the north of Italy with the whole of France still to cover before she gets home is not the ideal place for her to be when she finds out that I have to walk away.

I also can't arrive back in London with her, though; I feel like our real home lives should not collide.

The ideal location for us to part ways would be Paris, I realise. I can tell her I can't commit to any kind of relationship, because I don't want to keep on hurting her over and over again, and I think the sticking-plaster approach has to be the best one. I can make sure she's safely on her way back to London – I'm sure that, even at Emma's speed, it can't be that long a drive from Paris to Calais – and I'm sure it will be easy for me to find another transport option from there.

And before that, I will be careful not to pour out all the love and endearments that I want to lavish on her – I will do my best to make it clear that this is just for now – but, if she's also keen, I will enjoy these few days with her.

So I'll tell her about Thea when we get to Paris. And then I'll go.

God. Thea. I didn't call her yesterday. I messaged her but had no time to phone. That obviously does happen sometimes, but I hate it when it does.

It actually *never* happens because of a girlfriend; and that's just more proof that being with Emma causes me to behave differently and not necessarily well.

Which is further confirmation that we should not be together.

And now, decision made, I'm going to get on with enjoying every last moment with Emma until we part in Paris but first I think I have to be very explicit right now about the fact that this cannot be more than a holiday fling effectively. And if she then doesn't want to do anything intimate again I will obviously totally get that.

I wrap my arms fully around her, and she stirs and immediately turns her face up to mine. I kiss her and then I pull back a little, proud of myself as I do it, because obviously I don't want to say anything and spoil this moment, but also I do now have to be honest.

'I feel...' I begin. God. This is hard. Okay, just a couple of sentences. 'This is magical, amazing, wonderful. But I don't think...' Oh my *God* this is difficult. 'I think, for me, this, *us*, can only be for this trip.'

She stares into my eyes for what feels like minutes, and then she whispers, 'Okay.'

She's been in my arms the whole time. I tighten my grip on her and she wriggles so that her arms come round me and then she turns her face to mine and we kiss and kiss before making love like the end of the world's coming.

14

EMMA

Honestly, I'm not sure I've ever enjoyed waking up as much as I did this morning. For the first few seconds.

I was in a really deep sleep and had no idea where I was at first, other than *very* comfortable and *very* content, and then I began to remember – Callum, yesterday evening, last night, *Callum* – and then I realised that I was in his lovely strong arms and then I lifted my head and looked at him and then he kissed me.

And then he basically told me that from his side this is just a holiday fling.

Which... hurt, even though it wasn't new news. Except, because it wasn't new news, I realised, as I looked into his beautiful eyes, that it shouldn't have hurt me.

And, in the end, I thought that if that's all it is I'll take it, because saying goodbye to him – if that's what has to happen – will hurt no matter what. So I might as well enjoy myself with him while I can. And then, yes, lust did then take over. And I said okay.

And *then*... Oh. My. Goodness.

The best sex anyone's ever had in the history of the world ever.

And I'll just say it happened a lot more than once and leave it there.

I still feel like screaming out loud when I think about it.

Literally mind-blowing.

Afterwards, Callum was so gorgeous and lovely and cuddly and held me so tight that I did wonder whether maybe he didn't really mean what he said about it being just for now. Or maybe that's stupid wishful thinking, but whatever. For the moment, I have his company and his... well, it feels like love. Obviously it *isn't* love if he doesn't think this can be forever. But it's certainly very nice.

Now, we're sitting outside a beachfront café eating brunch – basically focaccia and salami with a *lot* of strong coffee – smiling soppily at each other and commenting lazily on what's in front of us.

'I wouldn't like to be a seagull,' I say. 'Just flying around and eating the whole time. I think it would be boring.'

'Better than being a goat, though,' Callum says very seriously, indicating the hillside in the distance behind, where we saw goats yesterday. 'They don't even get to fly and they just eat the same thing the whole time.'

'True. And flying would be cool,' I agree. 'And swooping. Spying and eavesdropping.'

'With their little seagull ears?'

'Exactly.' I think for a moment. 'I'd like to be an amazing mountain climber, though, like a goat.'

'That's a very good point. And they do always *look* happy.'

Our highly intellectual conversation wends its way through a lot of similarly highly intellectual conversational topics.

We don't mention anything serious or relationshippy at all again.

As Callum takes a final bite of a little raspberry tart, washes it down with coffee, and leans back in his chair with his legs stretched out, I reflect that, apart from his one comment about the fling when we woke up this morning, he shows no sign whatsoever of wanting to talk about real life.

And I actually also have no wish to go there.

Today feels too other-world perfect to spoil it with mundane matters like... this is my baggage, what's yours... or where are we *really* going, if anywhere, from here, like did you actually *mean* what you said before you then made love to me as though you were... yes, making *love*?

I know now without a shadow of a doubt – it's just come to me suddenly – where *I'd* like to go with Callum: marriage, kids, the works. And, yes, I've only re-known him for just over forty-eight hours (how is it even possible that it's been such a short time?), but we were together for three years and I know the bones of him, his personality, his temperament, his morals, *him*, so, so well. And I don't think I've ever stopped loving him.

I don't want to think about this. I don't want to contemplate Callum not feeling the same way.

I open my mouth to speak, to get away from my thoughts, just as Callum rolls his shoulders and says, 'Shall we get the bill and have a quick walk along the beach before we get going?'

'Good idea.' I beam. I love that word *we*.

As we stroll, hand in hand, I push away all thoughts about the future. I'm here with Callum and it's blissful, and I do at least now know why he didn't get back in touch and that in itself is huge. And at the very, very least, I'll have these few days as the most perfect memory. And maybe that *will* be all this is: a beautiful (and sex-filled) closure to a first love.

If so, that will be that and I'll have to accept it.

In this moment, I'm just going to enjoy myself with Callum.

I pull his hand. 'Let's paddle.'

* * *

We end up going into the sea in our clothes (and then if I'm honest doing some things that I never thought I'd do in the open air but there's no one around and I'm sure people can't see things under water – thank *goodness* there were no snorkellers) before lying on the sand to dry off and then going back to the van.

'Are we still thinking Chamonix for the next stop?' Callum asks as we set off.

'I've been wondering that myself,' I admit. 'How long's Google Maps saying?'

'Four hours forty-five minutes from here.'

'So realistically that's nine hours if we're lucky.'

I am not, it turns out, as fast on the motorway as sat navs predict that I will be. I've started doubling their estimates to be safe.

'Yeah.' Callum nods. And that's a testament to how good a mood he must be in today, because at any other time in the two days we've been on this trip together, he would immediately have made the point that if I drove faster we'd get places faster. Like: no shit, *really*? I'm *aware* that I'm not the fastest driver on the road. He's being a lot more tolerant now, and I like that.

'Maybe we should stop somewhere halfway between here and there. Where do you think would be good?'

I realise with a little shock that this is literally the first decision about this trip I'm asking someone else to help me make, and it feels good.

I was very ready to strike out by myself when I first set out, but now I'm very happy to have some company. Callum's company, anyway.

We decide to stop for the night just off the motorway in a

village in a forested national park in the foothills of the Alps, still in Italy.

Once we've made the decision, Callum says, 'I should book a hotel now while we're driving. We don't want to arrive and discover that there's nowhere to stay because it's a village with no hotels or there's just one and it's completely full.'

I agree and he does some googling.

'Okay, there are a few hotels in the vicinity. The nicest one does have space for us. I was thinking.' He clears his throat. 'In the interests of.' He clears his throat again.

I'm pretty sure that he's referring to how many bedrooms we book. I know what I'd like to do but I do *not* want to say, just in case it isn't what Callum's getting at.

And then he gets the words out: 'Would you like to share a room?'

I would *love* to share a room.

'Let me think about that,' I tease. 'Yeah, only if you promise to let me choose my side of the bed and also let me have as many bedclothes as I like.'

I get cold at night; Callum does not.

'*Or*,' he says, 'I could very kindly warm you up myself.'

'Oh yes, I think that could work very well. Done.'

He makes the booking and then we listen to music again, and sing, and Callum is indeed blatantly in an extremely tolerant mood, because he only mentions about five times, instead of about fifty, the fact that I do occasionally (all the time; I can't remember the words of songs to save my life) sing *la* a lot.

It's *so* nice. I love being in the van with him, bowling along the Italian motorway. It's like we're in a moving home, looking out on the rest of the world, just the two of us, bound together by proximity. (And love, at least in my case, but I don't want to go there.)

We don't talk a lot, we just sing and smile and occasionally comment vaguely on the scenery.

We stop once, and even a small service station with bad food and very smelly and not-very-clean loos seems like a lovely destination when I'm with Callum.

During the early evening, when we're still on the motorway, there's a brief but heavy rain shower.

'Just turning my windscreen wipers on.' I do it with a flourish.

'Nicely done. You wouldn't ever want to drive a wiper-less vehicle,' Callum says.

I smile. I love that we now have mild in-jokes from this trip. In many ways it's as though the last twelve years never happened – we've slipped so fast back into our old Callum-and-Emma, Emma-and-Callum relationship.

Actually, I don't think we've slipped back into our old relationship; I think this could be a *better* version. Every single evening from a couple of months in after we first met, when I'd realised that the one-offs were not actually one-offs, I always used to be a little bit worried that any minute Callum was going to do something truly outrageous. I don't have that fear now. He seems a *lot* more grown-up, in a very good way, and now obviously I do have the background fear that he's going to stick to his 'this is only for now' thing, but in the moment I'm just loving being with him. Maybe... if something longer term happens... maybe the break could have been a good thing (if a little long); maybe it allowed us both space to grow.

Callum is actually very good at giving directions from Google Maps (which is genuinely harder than you'd think based on how shockingly bad at it Samira was when she joined me for a week in Austria) and we reach the hotel without making any wrong turnings.

'Oh wow,' I say, when the very smiley owner shows us our room.

Callum's booked us a luxury suite, and there's a heavy emphasis on the *luxury*. Our room has a very large and comfortable four-poster bed, and everything (the bed included) is decorated in sumptuous pale blue and green velvets and silky fabric, with a pattern of tiny flowers, which goes beautifully with the dark blue walls and cream woodwork. We also have a sitting room, painted cream, containing a dark blue velvet sofa of the ideal squishiness, and a huge TV. Our en-suite bathroom is Paris-Ritz-style opulent, and goes perfectly with the cosy grandness of the room. And the view from the windows (on three sides because we're in a turrety bit of the building) is to die for: we can see the Alps stretching away into the distance, lots of grassy hillside with trees and bushes and the occasional village or hamlet dotted around.

'I love this.' I'm almost speechless with delight. 'I want to move in permanently. It's perfect.' This would be the most idyllic honeymoon location. And, oops, I hope I'm not blushing when I realise that being here with Callum has sent my thoughts straight to weddings and honeymoons.

The owner beams at me. 'I'm so pleased that you like it.' She points to a side table in the sitting room and says, 'We have champagne on ice for you. We can serve dinner downstairs in the dining room or we can do room service. Whichever you prefer?'

It's always nice to dine in a restaurant and meet new people, but on this occasion I would infinitely prefer to stay in the room and make the most of it... and more importantly of Callum. But he booked the hotel, having insisted again that he should be the one to pay, so it should be his decision.

'I think, perhaps, room service?' He's looking at me with his eyebrows raised in query. 'If you like? I'm very happy to go down to the restaurant if you prefer.'

'Room service would be perfect,' I say quickly, cheering internally.

We didn't have a lot to eat at the service station so we order starters, mains and dessert. We sit on our terrace and enjoy the view for the first two courses and we do actually eat them, but before we get to our dessert we're trying out the bed.

It's a good bed and we put it to excellent use.

Later, when we're wrapped in sheets, eating strawberries and delectable little biscuits, Callum kisses me on the mouth and says, 'I...' Followed by what I would swear sounds like an 'L' sound.

I wait, with bated breath, because for a moment I had a really strong sense that he might be about to say he loved me. But he doesn't say anything else; he kind of clamps his mouth shut. Which is fine. It's too soon. Probably.

Maybe in fact he wasn't about to say he loved me. The shape of his mouth, though, was definitely just like he was going to form the word 'love'. And I can't imagine he would have gone so weird in the moment if he'd been about to say a word that starts similarly.

I'm trying to think of sentences that he might feasibly have said that would start like that, like, 'I lump things together,' or 'I lunge when I'm exercising,' or... and then he takes both our bowls and kisses me really hard and hungrily, and I stop thinking about anything at all, including L words.

We wake up the next day having had an idyllic night in the idyllic surroundings we're in.

We share an idyllic room-service breakfast.

The whole day – our morning walking round the hotel's lovely gardens after we've got up very late, followed by a slow journey up to Chamonix through stunning Alpine scenery and the end of the afternoon and early evening walking around the picturesque town – is perfect.

We're very tactile the whole time, just as though we're a regular, very loved-up, couple.

We talk but we don't *talk*. It's all banter, little stories, some very naughty innuendos that make me go, '*Callum*,' before trying to beat him with some of my own. There's nothing deep and meaningful. Just like a solid, loved-up couple might be on holiday, because they know where they are with each other. And just like two people who are in a holiday fling might be because they know where they are too: nowhere.

We're walking through a little square, hand in hand, and I suddenly say, 'Oh my goodness, you've done no work all day. Will it not matter? Your job? Do you not have stuff you *have* to do?' And then I continue with: 'What *do* you actually do, in fact? In your law job?' Which doesn't feel like an intrusive question, because most people are perfectly happy to tell most other people what their jobs consist of. Like, for example, I must have collected (and mainly forgotten but that is not the point) details about at least twenty new acquaintances' occupations during the course of this trip.

Callum hesitates for just a second, but I notice the hesitation, because it seems odd.

And then he says, 'Yes, I'm a lawyer. Solicitor. I work for quite a big firm. In London.' Then he says, very, very much as though he's changing the subject, 'Wow, look at that view.'

And, yes, the view – of the snow-capped Mont Blanc – is stunning and absolutely comment-worthy but that was just weird. Why doesn't Callum want to talk about his job? Does he not want to share any details at all of his life with me? I mean, his *job*. That isn't even that personal. Now that I've re-met him and I know he's a lawyer, I could probably find him online quite easily. It isn't classified information. It's like his instinct is just to shut the conversation down when we get anywhere *near* personal.

No. This is ridiculous. I'm being paranoid. There's no *reason* that people should just info-dump on each other. And maybe he has a work issue that he just doesn't want to talk about, or he's feeling a bit worried about not having done any work and he wants to put it out of his mind and just enjoy our surprise holiday together. There could be all *sorts* of not-at-all-bad reasons that he doesn't want to discuss his job with me.

I look over at the mountains and agree that the view is spectacular and then we carry on wandering and I wonder whether I imagined things getting weird there for a moment.

* * *

Our night in Chamonix is perfect. As are the next two days and nights on the road.

It's like we're in an out-of-this-world bubble.

The bubble feeling is heightened because we obviously aren't seeing anyone we know, and I'm not really hugely in touch with anyone either; I do obviously check in with my mum and sister and best friends when they message me, but I almost consciously tailor my replies so that they give an impression of: 'I'm very busy having an amazing time and am certainly not having sex with the ex to end all exes, nothing to see here, and I'll be home in maybe a week's time and when I do get home I'll fill you in on all my touristy but not at all sexual experiences'.

Callum and I continue to talk a *lot* but not about big life issues, just a lot of very lovely nothing-chat, during which I feel, actually, that we're getting to know the real us even better. We knew each other well before, but that was the young us. The older us are the same people but with a lot more life experience and that makes a difference. And I continue to feel that we're *better* together now.

We discuss important things like why food *does* taste better if you're looking at a nice view (in my head *Callum* is the nicest view of all), whether it's okay to wear the same socks two days running if you only wear them for half an hour each time and keep them tucked inside your shoes the rest of the time (no it is not, Callum) and why we say Mont Blanc with no 'the', but the French call it Le Mont Blanc, and our discussions do grow heated, but we do not touch on *important* important issues.

On the second evening, the last before we head towards Paris, we stay in a B&B in Burgundy in the middle of the countryside. The owners cook dinner for all their guests every evening and we all eat together at a big table in their dining room.

Their fifteenth-century manor house is very well-loved and stuffed full of objects collected by their family over many years. Someone at some point in their history has had a big leaning towards taxidermy, with a particular emphasis on birds, and (a little weirdly) there's a whole row of them (quite small ones, mainly with very beady eyes) down the middle of the big oak dining table, which does put you off your food a bit until you get used to them.

'Can anyone identify any of these birds?' asks the Belgian man to my left.

We all start with guesses like 'robin' and 'blue tit' but none of us are remotely expert in birds, it turns out. Callum and I, together with a couple of the others, begin to invent names like 'Burgundian red-cheeked tit' and 'long-beaked jade bird' and, even though we aren't being at *all* witty, we do find ourselves very amusing, I think because the atmosphere of the room is just lovely and we're all in various different stages of holiday (our host instructed us at the beginning of the meal to break the ice by sharing how we came to stay here).

I catch Callum's eye as we're both laughing and think how this is exactly the kind of conversation we have when it's just the two of us and it's lovely that we can have it in a group, too.

When we've all (literally) wiped our eyes and stopped holding our sides, the Belgian man's husband (they're on a road-trippy honeymoon, on their way to the Italian lakes) asks me about where we went in Italy.

I can't help *loving* the assumption that everyone's making that Callum and I are a long-standing couple (and in a way we are, because when you knew each other very, very well as young adults you do properly *know* each other, maybe not the minutiae of everyday life today, but you know each other's personalities and temperaments and morals and, just, *bones*).

We begin to talk about Florence, and then the woman opposite me, who's *called* Florence, says, 'Funny thing: I've been to Sienna, but I've never been to Florence, but I feel a connection to it, just because of my name.'

'Oh, you *have* to go,' I say. And then feel guilty, because you never know about people's circumstances. 'If you get the opportunity, I mean.' Then I frown. 'Isn't it weird how Sienna and Florence are both very well-known Christian names but Milan and Venice aren't. How did that happen?'

As we all start to very seriously discuss place names that are Christian names and which would make good ones (why is no one called Ljubljana or Helsinki, for example), I see Callum smiling at me in the exact same way that he smiles at me when we're alone having this kind of conversation.

And suddenly something ice-cold curls around my happiness as though it's trying to suffocate it. Because should we be able to have the exact same conversations with or without other people?

When you're talking to someone who you're having a lot of deep and meaningful (and also just physically glorious) sex with and rebuilding a serious relationship with them, shouldn't you at least sometimes go more personal than you would with other people?

I suppose the *sex* is a physical kind of conversation that we clearly wouldn't involve anyone else in. But shouldn't we be having some *spoken* conversations that could only be for us?

I take a deep, steadying breath as unease seems to flood my whole body and for a moment I feel very light-headed and almost as though I might faint despite the very solid chair I'm on.

And then I look again at Callum's laughing face and I remember that this is a stolen holiday for him and we're away from home and that – if we're going to continue this (I hope so much that we will even though I know he did say this could only be a fling) – things will be very different when we're back in London and in each other's *real* lives. This *is* a holiday and it's nice to have an escape from real life and it's great actually that we're keeping everything so light. We have an undercurrent of seriousness and that's enough for me.

In fact, it's probably a *nice* thing that we aren't one of those couples who can *only* be together; we can have a really good time in a group.

The rest of the evening is lovely and our night in yet another grand four-poster bed is *amazing.* (We pull the bed's curtains around us because neither of us fancies being watched by the stuffed rodents that are crowded onto every conceivable surface and very much not my favourite form of taxidermy.)

* * *

It's quite late when we arrive in Paris on the third day.

'I'm agog to see what else you booked,' I say, as Callum directs me into one of the few car parks in Central Paris that the van will fit into height-wise.

He asked me this morning if he could book a surprise evening for us and I said yes, that would be lovely, and in the last few minutes, when I've had any time around dodging the *scary* traffic, I've been wondering in a lovely anticipatory way what we're going to be doing.

When we emerge blinking from the greyness of the car park into the bright late afternoon light, Callum says, 'The hotel's just round the corner.'

'That's so close.'

I'm very impressed.

'Oh my goodness,' I say a minute later when we get round the corner and see the hotel. It's in a very historic-looking building, with a big revolving door with a liveried man standing outside. It's all very black and gold and shiny. There are well-kept window boxes containing gorgeous bright purple and red flowers. There's classic-but-discreet lettering. It's *so* fancy.

We're ushered inside by the liveried man and over to the polished dark wood reception desk. Inside, there's a lot of gold and shiny marble floor tiles and panelled walls. You'd think it would be overwhelming, but it isn't; it's just gorgeous.

'This is lovely,' I say.

'I know.' Callum's smug smile is very endearing. 'Wait until you see the pool.' He did suggest that I put a costume in the bag I packed for tonight, so I did think there might be a pool but I did *not* think the hotel would be like *this*.

The bedroom is more of the same classic luxury. (Since the first time we shared, we've been in the same room every night as a matter of course without even discussing it.)

The first thing we do, after we've bounced a bit on the bed (and then stolen a quick cuddle) and exclaimed about the very fancy bathroom and exclusive view over a very beautiful square, is go for a swim in the rooftop infinity pool.

After a few lengths and some messing around with Callum, I climb out to have a little rest on one of the loungers. I wrap myself in one of the super-deep-pile towels they've provided for guests and lie back and watch him.

These past few days we've seen a lot of amazing scenery and wonderful architecture, as well as some cool, quirky things, some of which I won't necessarily ever have the opportunity to see again, and most of the time I've had to force myself to look at the sights rather than at Callum. The actual real-life thing of not being able to get enough of someone.

As I watch him now, he's powering through the pool in a very efficient front crawl, and I feel myself shivering with pleasure at the thought that I get to spend all this time with him, be with him, talk to him, *love* him.

He executes a very professional-looking turn at the end of his lap; he's *good*.

Did I know he was such a good swimmer? I'm not sure I did. Now I think about it, I don't think we ever went proper swimming in the three years we were together – well, we can't have done; I would have remembered – and I thought he only did football and tennis, sports-wise.

I like that we still have stuff like this to learn about each other. What I don't like so much, I realise, is that we still haven't caught up on all the big life stuff that's happened over the past twelve years, and I feel as though it's more Callum than me now stopping us from having those conversations.

But maybe he's right. Maybe that would spoil this holiday together.

We can talk about it all when we get back to London. I am now, I realise, pretty sure that we're going to be together when we get home. I know that Callum said that definitely wouldn't be the case, but that was before we'd spent so much amazing time together.

I think maybe he was scared that one – or both – of us would get hurt and that's why he said the fling thing, but surely now he can see that that wouldn't be the case. I mean, we are *good* together.

'Come back in for a few more minutes?' Callum calls and I nod and stand up, before sliding back into the pool and stopping with the thinking.

After our swim, we shower (together) in our en-suite, and then I put on my favourite dress (Callum said we're going to eat dinner somewhere nice) and almost skip downstairs with him due to the happiness practically bubbling out of me.

He's organised the most wonderful evening. I told him a few days ago about how the only other time I've been to Paris I was fourteen and on a school trip and missed everything that the teachers had arranged for us because I spent most of it being sick in the bathroom in our youth hostel after a dodgy chicken sandwich on the ferry. So he's booked us into some touristy things.

We take a *bateau mouche* along the river, we wander the historic streets and I do actually take my eyes off Callum long enough to fall in love with Paris too, and then we take a cab to the Eiffel Tower, where Callum's booked for us to have dinner in the second-floor restaurant, from where the views are fantastic.

Over dinner we again talk about everything but also, as usual, it's very much nothing.

And then, as we sip coffees and eat the most amazing little truffle chocolates, Callum puts his cup down and leans in.

He looks me very intently in the eyes, and I suddenly get the feeling that he's about to say something that's a lot more everything than nothing. I put my own cup down.

'Emma, you need to know that I love you,' he says, taking both my hands in his. 'More than words can ever say.'

My heart makes the most gigantic leap inside me, almost into my mouth.

'I love you too,' I tell him. I'm bordering on tearful. There isn't a shadow of a doubt in my mind that I love him, deeply, irrevocably, forever. I recovered from him, eventually, after the end of our relationship, and I moved on, but now I know that I never stopped loving him, I just learned to live without him. And now I think I've unlearnt that, very fast. 'I'm so glad that we re-met like this.'

Callum – a little bit weirdly – doesn't reply, but maybe he's just struggling to find words around the emotion we're both feeling. That must be it; I see his Adam's apple working as he sits there silently and his eyes moisten a tiny bit. I can feel tears spiking at the backs of my own eyes, and I sniff.

I'm opening my mouth to say what a wonderful evening this has been (and probably something else about loving Callum because it's the kind of sentiment that you can't stop repeating once you've started it) when the moment is annoyingly broken as I'm clunked on the head by the very weighty handbag of the woman on the next table as she stands to leave. (What does she *have* in there? I honestly think it must be a *gun* or something.)

'Ow.' I'm no longer gazing into Callum's eyes; I'm slightly seeing stars.

'Shall we get the bill?' Callum asks and I nod, suddenly keen to get back to the hotel and be alone and cement our declaration by making love, which I think will be huge, given that it's the first time since we reconnected that we've *told* each other we love each other.

We walk back to the hotel with our arms round each other. It's quite a long walk but it passes quickly. We talk a bit, about things like gargoyles on buildings and famous places that we pass, the bakeries, chocolateries and macaron shops, with their saliva-inducing displays, and amazing little shops, like one that's entirely devoted to stunning ribbons, and we also wander in silence at times, during which all I think about is the fact that we've now told each other that *we love each other*.

* * *

When we wake up in the morning, I feel normal at first, and then I feel the weight of Callum spooned round me and I remember last night, and I don't feel normal any more; I feel like the luckiest woman alive. I lie there just *smiling*.

But then, instead of kissing me or doing any of the other things that he's been doing when we wake up each morning, Callum clears his throat behind me. It's a weird throat-clearing for the situation we're in. It's the kind of throat-clearing you do when you have something to say in a work meeting or something. You wouldn't think a throat-clearing sound could alarm you, but I do feel a little alarmed.

'Callum?' I ask.

'I need to get back to London,' he says. 'Fast. A work thing. There's a train from the Gare du Nord late morning today, and my PA's booked me onto it. I just found out.'

'Oh.' I feel instantly incredibly deflated but then I think no, that's okay. He wasn't expecting to be on holiday at all, so we've been very lucky to have this time together. Obviously it was always going to be finite. We can just see each other when I get back, whenever we're both free. Hopefully sooner rather than later but we do both have our own lives. The main thing is that we love each other and I'm sure we're going to find a way to join our actual lives, not just our holiday lives, together.

'So I'm just going to get into the shower.' He pulls his arms from round me and as he gets out of bed he doesn't kiss me, which feels a bit (very) odd, but he's clearly in a rush, which is totally understandable.

I enjoy watching him walk naked across the room to the bathroom. It's a view you could happily see every day for the rest of your life. And, oh my goodness, hopefully I will. He's changed a little from how he was when we were young, as I have. I want to see all the rest of the changes; I want to grow middle-aged with him and then old with him. I want him in my life forever.

I drift back into sleep thinking of Callum.

I think the sound of the bathroom door opening wakes me up; I'm disorientated again for a moment when I re-wake, and then face-splittingly-wide-smiled happy when I remember.

Me and Callum. Callum and me. We're in love.

Callum's in a suit.

'Suits you, sir,' I say, still smiling.

He doesn't smile back and my own smile starts to drop. He's looking... *odd*. Like, quite frowny. Oh my God. Is he regretting telling me that he loved me? Did he not... *mean* it?

I swallow. I can barely deal with all the terror I'm feeling right now. Does he *not* want to see me again when we're both back in London?

And then he sits down on the bed. At the other end. Beyond my feet.

And he says, 'I have something to tell you.'

His face is very serious and I know beyond a shadow of a doubt that I am not going to enjoy hearing whatever he has to say.

15

CALLUM

I am such a fucking idiot.

I should have had myself under better control last night.

What the fuck was I thinking telling Emma that I love her? Obviously I *do* love her. But – without being conceited – it's clear that she also loves me, and that is not a good thing. I'm pretty sure that she's going to be very hurt now and I'm guessing – well, certain – that the exchange of I-love-yous will not have helped. Again, without being conceited, I think there's every chance that she was beginning to hope or plan for a proper relationship, and obviously my behaviour last night implied that I was too.

I should not have said it.

'Yes?' Her voice is the sharpest I've ever heard it and the sound breaks my heart.

I've done that to her. We've spent an idyllic few days together and – instigated by me – we've said we love each other, and now I'm doing this.

Maybe she'll begin to hate me. She isn't the kind of person who hates people. I will have done that to her. It might be a good thing in the short term, so that she can move on with her life without me, but I don't think it's healthy to learn to hate people. I'll have damaged her. Which perfectly demonstrates why this is the right decision.

I should have walked away at the beginning, though. I should not have got sucked into any of this.

When Janet told me a couple of days ago that she could get me on a train from Lyon to London, I should not have said, 'do you know what, I'm good with my lift', I should have bloody said thank you so much to Janet and goodbye then and there to Emma, instead of saying nothing about anything to Emma and carrying on with the charade.

I wanted to stay with Emma partly, obviously, because I was loving her company, but partly also as a companion for her because I was worried about her travelling alone, but in reality she'd have been absolutely fine like she has been for the rest of the trip. I'm not sure whether I was being a patronising idiot or whether I was using the worry about her safety as an excuse for staying with her.

Whichever, I should, basically, have gone for the sticking-plaster approach a lot sooner. And, having not done it then, I should at least learn from my mistake and do it now.

So I'm going to dive straight in.

'I shouldn't have told you I love you,' I begin, and oh fuck, the look on her face; it kills me to see it. Just immediately broken. 'Not because I don't love you, because I do,' and oh fuck now she looks confused rather than heartbroken, I need to just *get on with it*, 'but because we can't go anywhere. We can't have a relationship. I cannot be with you. So I shouldn't have said it.'

Emma doesn't speak immediately. She presses her lips together and looks up at the ceiling instead of at me.

And then she swallows, and says, 'I see.'

I close my eyes for a moment, because suddenly my eyelids feel incredibly heavy, as though they're weighted down by tears that I am not going to be selfish enough to allow myself to shed. Then I open them and say, 'I'm so sorry.'

Emma does a little nod, and then she shuffles herself up the bed, the sheets drawn very tightly round her nakedness, over her chest, and sits up against her pillows.

'For me,' she says, speaking very slowly, 'I thought a few days ago that it was a very good thing to have seen you again, so that I could understand what happened all those years ago when you never came back to me. I was grateful to have had the opportunity to have got that closure. Well, it felt like closure. Now it feels as though I've had a deep wound reopened. So I'd be very grateful for proper closure. I would very much like to know why you can't be with me so that I can understand everything and not spend any more time ever again wondering about you.' Her words could be construed as angry, but I think she's just deeply sad, just stating out loud how she feels.

'Yep, I get that.'

'Soooo?' She looks slightly impatient, which is an improvement on devastation.

Of course I owe her a full explanation.

'There's someone else.'

There's a long pause during which Emma just stares at me, frowning, her mouth slightly open.

And then she sits up straight.

'There is *what*? You *arsehole*. You know, that's the one thing I never suspected you of. You *tosser*. You've been sleeping with me while you have a *partner*. You *arse*. You stupid, horrible, two-timing bastard. Your poor partner. You shit.'

'No, no, no.' Why did I word it like that? What's wrong with me? 'Not another woman. I have a daughter.'

'What?' Emma's jaw almost hits her chest.

'The first woman I was with after we split up – a long time afterwards, over a year later – got pregnant. We didn't have a relationship. We'd broken up – I mean, it wasn't even a break-up because we weren't even together – before she found out she was pregnant. So, yes, I have a daughter. Thea.'

'Oh.' She just stares at me.

'I'm so sorry for not having mentioned her before now.' I feel as though I ought also to apologise for the upset that Thea's existence is clearly causing Emma, but I can't do that; I could never be anything other than infinitely grateful to have my daughter.

'Yep.' Emma pulls the sheet more firmly around herself and sits up even more upright. 'I don't even know where to start.'

'I'm sorry,' I repeat.

'Yeah.' She's clearly beginning to gather her thoughts. 'Small things first: a year wasn't that long; I waited for you for *three* years, because I did not actually know that we had definitely split up. Also: the whole "we didn't have a relationship" thing? That you had – didn't have – with Thea's mother? I'm thinking that maybe that's what you and I have had this week, without me realising. A lot of sex, no relationship. And the big thing: *you have a daughter*. We've spent nearly a week together; we've done so much together. We've talked; we've just been so *together*. I thought we were *making love*, not just shagging like pathetic rabbits. How could you not have mentioned her?'

'I didn't want to hurt you.'

As I say it, I realise it's one of the most stupid things anyone has ever said.

Emma pulls the sheets hard, and then indicates where I'm sitting with an eyebrow-raise.

'Sorry, sorry.' I stand up hurriedly and she pulls the sheets even further around herself and then leans back against the headboard.

'You can sit down again if you like,' she says.

'I'm fine,' I say, trying to be polite.

'I would *like* you to sit down. I am wearing only a sheet and therefore have to stay in bed, and it is not pleasant being loomed over.'

'Of course.' I sit back down so fast that the whole bed rocks a little when I make contact.

'I would still be grateful if I could get the full facts from you so that I have actual closure,' she tells me. 'I'm assuming we won't be seeing each other again and I don't want to be lying awake at night wondering anything. Being selfish.'

'That is not selfish.'

I want to hug her so very, very much, but I know it's the last thing I should do.

'Thank you.' She doesn't smile. 'How old is Thea?'

'Ten.'

'Where does she live?'

'London.'

'Was she a contributory factor in you sorting yourself out and getting your law job?'

'Nope. That was all because of you. Although obviously she's an incredibly strong impetus for me to live the best life I can now.' I realise as Emma flinches that that sounds awful; it sounds as though my best life could not include her. 'My best life *would* include you,' I hasten to clarify. And then I realise that that was yet another spectacularly stupid thing to say. 'But I can't be with you.'

'Right.' She looks at me for a long moment, her features rigid, and then asks, 'Because of Thea?'

I shake my head, mutely.

'So why can you not be with me?' She pauses and I see her swallow and I feel my eyes heat with tears that I cannot be self-indulgent enough to shed. 'Sorry, that sounded ridiculous. If you don't want to be with me then you should not be with me. Obviously. I would never, ever wish to make anyone be with someone they don't want to be with. You don't want to be with me. I understand that that is a fact and I do of course accept it.'

Fuck. I *hate* her dignity. I'd rather she be really angry and shouty.

'But,' she continues, 'I would like, if you're able to tell me, to know *why* you feel you don't want to be with me. Because we *were* together for a long time, and I always felt that we would have stayed together if I hadn't lost it and been unable to deal any more with your wildness. I thought that *if* you sorted yourself out you'd come back. But you didn't, and then we met again and I feel as though we fell in love all over again this week, but you don't want to be with me and I suppose I would just like to know the reason for that. Not because I'm trying to change your mind – because I wouldn't like to do that. I would only want someone to want to be with me because they *wanted* to.'

I can see out of the corner of my eye the clock on the mantelpiece. I know it's right because I looked at it yesterday evening when we were going out. The clock tells me that if I don't leave pretty much now I'm going to struggle to make my train.

I owe this to Emma, though. I love her. I want to upset her as little as possible. I want her to have her closure and never think about me again. And oh God it *hurts* to think of her not thinking of me again. But that would be best for her.

'I don't want to hurt you,' I say.

'Right.' Her eye-roll comforts me a little, the fact that she's capable of something more than total grief right now. I just cannot bear to ruin her life.

'The reason that I cannot be with you is that I cannot bear to hurt you.'

Emma just raises her eyebrows.

'I never stay with any woman for long,' I try to explain. 'When I was young I was beyond stupid, as we know. I wreck things. I wreck relationships. I wreck other people's happiness. I don't want to do that to you. It's like... it's like when I'm happy I begin to do things that destroy it. And that hurts people. And I never want to hurt you.'

'You're hurting me now.'

'Yes, but when I leave, you'll get over me.'

'Like I got over you last time?' Emma claps her hand over her mouth. 'I shouldn't have said that. I'm so sorry. I do not want to emotionally blackmail you into staying with me.'

'You aren't,' I say. She isn't, because my mind is made up.

'I don't really understand what you're talking about,' she says.

'It's hard to articulate.'

It is. It's very clear in my head but I just can't say it right, no matter how many times I try.

'Can I ask one more question?'

'Of course.' I take another surreptitious glance at the clock. Yep. Going to miss the train.

'Why now? Why did you wait until now? Why did we have this week together?' A single tear trickles down her cheek and I hate myself so much.

'Because I'm a stupid, stupid idiot,' I tell her. 'Initially I didn't realise what was happening. And then I thought... I don't know what I thought. I think I thought that once we'd started it wouldn't make it any worse to carry on for a bit longer because the hurt would already be there.'

She stares at me. 'You know what I want to say now? But I shouldn't?'

I shake my head. I think I *do* know but again I'm not doing well with articulating things.

'Why leave *now* is what I mean. Why not finish this next week or next year or next decade? Why not, for the moment, give it a go and just see what happens?'

'Oh, okay.' I think I know the answer to this. 'Because I know that at some point I'll fuck up and hurt you and it will all end and I'll be hurt too, which I won't enjoy. But the worst thing will be that I've let you down and you're hurt, and I don't want to be in a relationship with you knowing that you're investing in something that at some point I'm going to destroy. So I think we should stop now. Basically, I don't want to hurt you.'

'You mean like you're doing now?' she questions.

'Exactly. Like now.'

'And did you just hear what we both just said?' She has this heartbreaking little frown on her face, like she's puzzled.

'Yes.' I nod to confirm.

She looks at me for a long time and then says... 'So that's... that?'

'Yes.'

'Okay. Well. You should go and get your train then.' She has tears rolling down both cheeks now. I would like so much to wipe them away for her. I would like even more not to be the person who caused them. And for her never to have needed to cry over me.

It would have been so much better if we'd never met.

Although then we'd never have had the magical times we've had together.

Although the magic is pretty tarnished by splitting.

I don't know. I do not know anything.

I stand up and take the handle of my case and say, 'Goodbye. I'm so, so sorry.'

And I leave without looking back.

* * *

I do miss my train because it's busy on the Eurostar today, and the staff are impervious to my pleas. There are no seats free anywhere, so I sit on my case and think about what a fucking idiot I am and about the trainwreck of my life. And that is why I've done the right thing, because this is apparently what I do when I'm around Emma, I wreck stuff.

I look at the duty-free shop next to me. I'm tempted to buy myself a bottle of Jack Daniel's and down the whole lot.

I make the best decision I've made all week and buy myself a bottle of lemonade instead.

And then I carry on sitting on my case and try not to think about Emma.

16

EMMA

Mid-afternoon, I decide that I should eat something, so I tear off a piece of my croissant and put it in my mouth.

I'm sure I would have thought it was delicious twenty-four hours ago. Now it just tastes of grease. It's like the food equivalent of my 'relationship' with Callum over the past week: depending on how you look at it, it could be a wonderful experience, flooding my senses with its amazing smell and taste, warming me, filling me, or it could just be really bad for me and best left well alone, with no nutritional value whatsoever.

I put the rest of the croissant back in its paper bag and scrunch the opening.

I'm sitting on Paris Plage, the urban beach on the banks of the River Seine. It's a thirty-two-degree, not-a-cloud-in-the-sky day and I'm surrounded by chattering families, happy-looking couples, groups of friends. There's the occasional person sitting on their own, like me, reading or scrolling through their phone. I wonder if any of them just got their heart broken.

I *sobbed* in the shower – huge, fat, chest-heaving tears – and then I hauled myself and my case to the van and then – standing there in that car park feeling like total crap – I decided that I was not going to leave Paris before I'd seen some of it by myself.

This is, objectively, a beautiful city. I'd like to experience more of it. I'd like *not* to have my memories of it wrecked by Callum.

I mean, I *will* always think of him in Paris, obviously. But I would like to be able to come back here and see more of the city and *enjoy* being here.

So I decided to go for a walk. And then I thought I might be hungry – I said thank you but no thank you to Callum's offer of room-service breakfast in the hotel (I feel *rubbish* in hindsight about staying with him in all those lovely hotels, paid for by him) – so I bought a croissant because I found myself just *staring* at the various panini and baguette choices and realised that choosing sandwich fillings was one decision too many for me today.

And here I am, holding my greasy croissant bag, hiding my misery under my thankfully large and very dark sunglasses.

A couple maybe fifteen feet to my right suddenly make a commotion: it's a man and a woman, of around my age, and she's flung her arms round his neck while screaming and he has his face buried in her hair and is swinging her round and round, her feet off the ground.

He puts her down after a lot of swinging, perhaps a minute – how are they not now falling over? They must have *excellent* balance – and they stand together, arms round each other, beaming.

Maybe they've just got engaged or agreed to move in together or decided to try for a baby.

All things that I am never going to do with Callum.

I am such an idiot thinking this could work out. I've had so many stupid happily-ever-after fantasies over the past few days.

What. An. Idiot.

There were a lot of clues. Like the fact that he *told* me in the caravan that he couldn't commit. And my own unease in Burgundy.

I think back to when Callum told me he loved me in the Eiffel Tower restaurant. I didn't think about the wording or the sound of his declaration, the way his voice cracked; all I heard was the *I love you*. Because I'm stupid and I *wanted* to hear it and I did *not* want to question the love.

Thinking about it, Callum didn't make any promises. He was – I now realise with hindsight – very careful *not* to do that.

I feel a tear begin to trickle down behind my sunglasses. And then another.

Eurgh. I'm startled out of my self-absorption by a pigeon landing close to me, followed by another, attracted I think by a discarded baguette end. I really don't like being that close to birds.

These pigeons are *so* accustomed to humans.

I think about talking to Callum on the beach about birds, and sniff.

I said then that I wouldn't like to be a bird, and I'm sticking with that. I'd be really bored.

I love being a human. There's so much we can do.

And we only get one life.

And what am I *doing*, shaping up to waste *more* of my one life pining over Callum?

I'm not going to do it. I'm not going to pine.

I'm going to thank him in his absence for the great conversation and the company on the journey and the amazing sex and the very competent map reading and the lovely hotels and dinners. I'm going to chalk it up to life experience and I'm going to be *happy*. Entirely without him. This time, I *do* have closure and I'm going to do what you're supposed to do with closure: grab hold of it and move forward with your life.

I'm going to find myself a cheap hotel for tonight and do some sightseeing for the rest of today and tomorrow morning, and then I'm going to drive back home.

And when I get home, I'm going to organise lots of things with my friends. Maybe I'll take up some new hobbies, like padel tennis or Zumba. Maybe something creative like pottery. And I'm definitely going to do some more travelling in the future. There's a lot to look forward to. Beginning with the christening I'm going to on Sunday in the Cotswolds. I'm going to be godmother and it will be lovely to see everyone there.

Wow, I realise I didn't even tell Callum about that. We literally did not even talk about immediate weekend plans after we got back. We know *nothing* about each other's lives now.

The signs were all there. It was just a holiday fling.

And I'm going to be *fine.*

In the spirit of being fine, I'm going to get back on top of my admin before finding a hotel and maybe going to the Louvre or another museum this afternoon. Also, scrolling through my phone is quite a good distraction.

Looking through my messages, I remember that I got a text from Dev a couple of days ago – when Callum and I were in Chamonix, behaving practically like a honeymoon couple, what an *idiot* I was – and I didn't read it because I wanted to stay in my cocoon.

I've actually been neglecting all my friends and family, I realise, barely replying to any messages over the past few days.

Which in practice doesn't matter, because even though it's seemed like a long time and it feels to me as though so much has happened, it has in fact only been just over a week, so they won't really have noticed. But what it does indicate is that I have been ridiculous. It's like I just walked out of my real life to spend the week with Callum and that is not a sensible thing to do.

I'm too hot. I'm going to go to a café to eat a proper lunch and look through my messages and emails properly then.

Half an hour later, I'm sitting at a table under an awning outside a café with a view over the river, waiting for a tuna niçoise salad, and I open Dev's message.

I find myself frowning and blinking at what I see. I'm feeling a bit more together now I've had some lemonade – I honestly think I was in physical as well as mental shock and needed something sugary – and I didn't struggle *too* much with deciding on my lunch (helped by going for the set menu, which only has three main options) but I'm struggling to compute Dev's words.

He says he's in Paris for work for a few days and he'd like to meet up if I'm still going to be here at the end of my trip. He says he's really missed me, and to give him a call if I would like, and he would *really* like to see me.

I laugh out loud at the sheer ridiculousness of the timing, and the woman on the table next to me smiles across at me and in an American accent says, 'I'd like to read what you're reading.'

'Ha,' I reply, thinking: *No, you really would not.*

The waiter puts my salad down in front of me while I'm still staring at my phone and I pick up my cutlery.

By the time I've finished the salad, I've recovered my wits and I've done some thinking and I've decided to meet Dev.

I wanted closure with Callum and I got it. I don't really feel like I need closure from Dev, but maybe he feels like he needs closure from me. We were together for two years. And we were a big part of each other's lives during that time.

I should meet him.

He replies immediately when I text, and we agree to meet at the Musée d'Orsay in the middle of the afternoon. It's my suggestion because it's a museum full of really famous impressionist art that I'd like to see and if things feel awkward between us we'll have the art to talk about.

And, wow... I think, for me, it's going to be good seeing Dev. He's part of my real life; we aren't together any more but we were recently – as adults (as opposed to Callum and me when we were young) – and we share friends and recent knowledge about each other. This week with Callum has been a weird throwback fantasy and it will be good to put a layer of real life over my memories of him. And hopefully Dev will enjoy seeing me too, and we'll both have a good afternoon.

* * *

Dev and I agree to meet next to a statue of an elephant outside the museum, and, after a bit of confusion where I don't check the enormous statue I'm standing next to properly and spend *ages* waiting next to a rhino and we have to exchange calls to find each other, even though we've been standing only about twenty feet apart for a good ten minutes, we finally see each other.

My heart doesn't jump in the way it's always done when I've seen Callum, but I do actually feel pleased to see cheerily smiling, friendly, classically handsome, gorgeously uncomplicated Dev.

I've been travelling for four months now, and I realise that I'm ready to go home and be back in my real life, and I'm not really up any more for spending too much time sightseeing alone.

Also, Dev's always nice to me. He's pleasant company – quite often great company in fact – just *nice*.

'Hey.' He envelops me in a big bear hug and I cling to him for a moment, kind of for comfort, until I feel guilty that the reason that I need the comfort is Callum, and he is another man, and even though Dev and I split up and for all I know he's met any number of women since then, I think he might be – would be – hurt that the Callum thing has knocked me a lot more than splitting up with him did.

I pull back and smile at him. 'Hey.'

'Good to see you know your elephants from your rhinos.'

'Ha, yes.' I keep on smiling. I'm *very* pleased to see him, I realise. 'Shall we go in?'

We chat about what Dev's been up to (the usual basically, but he always has some good stories) and about my travels. Obviously I don't talk about Callum, because, well, I just can't right now, plus it clearly wouldn't be appropriate to talk to Dev about him.

We're looking at Monet's *Water Lilies* when I say, 'Did you know that he painted the same scenes so many times due to an ambition to document the French countryside across different seasons?'

And Dev replies, 'I really miss you. Would you... consider getting back together?'

I... What? What did he just say?

I feel my eyes swivelling left and right in shock as I keep my head pointed straight ahead at the painting.

Eventually, I ask, 'What did you say exactly?'

'Sorry, yes, sorry, that was pretty out of the blue. I just... I miss you so much, Emma, and seeing you... I'd love to get back together. It doesn't matter that you don't want to marry me.'

God. I give him a small smile and then look back at the painting again and try to think. My instinct is a big fat 'no, of course not; there's a reason that we split up'. But I don't feel that my instincts have served me well recently. I should try to analyse this.

Dev would never hurt me the way Callum did, because he *can't*. Because I do love him, of course I do – you never stop completely loving someone you used to love if there's no good reason to stop, and in our case when he asked me to marry him I just felt as though I shouldn't because it was like I needed something more –

something indefinable – and that's why we split up – but I don't love him in the same stupid, self-destructive, all-in way I love Callum. I know that because when we split up, the biggest thing that upset me about our big conversation was that I thought Dev was right when he very politely and kindly said could he just mention that he worried I didn't seize the day enough. And the reason I thought that he was right was that I've had an underlying worry through the whole of the past twelve years about that very same thing because of Callum.

I keep on staring at the lilies.

Maybe what this road trip has done is prove to me that I need to grow up. Stop with the hankering over what can never be. I want kids. I know that Dev wants kids. We're nice to each other. He's never hurt me and never would because he's a generous, kind, considerate, lovely man. Maybe this trip has taught me that I need to be pragmatic. I could have a lovely life with Dev.

Seize the day.

That's what I was doing when I set off on this trip so spontaneously.

Maybe, when you grow up, you have to learn that there are different kinds of seizing the day.

I think about the painting in front of me. Great painters have to seize the day, follow their passion, do what's right for them.

There's a lesson there.

I've come to a snap decision, I realise.

I turn to Dev.

17

CALLUM

It's the Sunday after I got back from France, and I'm standing with Thea in a beautiful old church in a chocolate-box-perfect Cotswold village, about to take part in the christening of my soon-to-be god-daughter Rose, Azim's baby girl. Azim's wife, Becca, grew up in this village, and wanted to have the christening here so that her elderly grandparents could come, so most of us have come here from London, and a few from other parts of the country.

I'm extremely honoured to have been asked to be godfather to Rose, and I'm grateful to be here in the Cotswolds. It feels such a world away from Italy and France that it's almost easy to pretend that my trip with Emma never happened, or that it was a very long time ago, so overall I'm feeling a little better than I was.

'Hugely relieved that you could make it,' Azim tells me. 'We were having nightmares about having to postpone it. You wouldn't believe how chocka this church's christening schedule is. When's Emma getting here?'

'Emma?' I query, confused. Is he talking about *Emma* Emma? He must be. But why? Why would he think that I would bring her? Or that she would be coming at all?

'Emma Milligan. Emma who you have just driven across Europe with.'

'She's coming?' I ask. 'To the christening?'

Damn. *Damn*. I should have thought of this. Azim is after all the person who put me in touch with Emma for the lift.

Azim doesn't have a chance to reply, because, as he's about to speak, Becca screams, 'Ems,' in a particularly piercing voice, thrusts Rose into Azim's arms, and sprints (as fast as someone can in a very tight knee-length dress and skyscraper-high heels) down the church path to launch herself into a huge hug with... Emma.

Emma Emma.

For the second time in under two weeks, I'm standing staring in her direction with no ability to think anything other than *what the actual...*

I feel as though fate's having a laugh at my expense right now. A nasty laugh. Or Azim is.

'How did you two get on?' Azim asks me. 'Becca and I thought you might... you know.' He does an exaggerated nudge and wink as my jaw hits the ground.

I'm pretty sure that he's just effectively told me that he and Becca tried to set me and Emma up. Owing to my mind being too stunned to work properly, I can't work out the implications of that, but my gut tells me that it really can't be good, given that she's *here*. I kind of want to discuss what he said with Emma, and dissect it with her, but of course I can't do that, because Emma and I aren't going to see each other ever again.

Except, here we are. Here Emma is.

She's now standing in front of me, her mouth in an O shape, staring at me just as much as I'm staring at her.

All of a sudden, I'm incredibly tired. I can't think beyond the very basic. In this case, the basics are that Emma has very nice shiny orangey lipstick on her O-shaped mouth, and she must be wearing heels as high as Becca's because her head's higher than usual. Oh yes, and she's *here*. That's the biggest basic.

'So Emma, you obviously know Callum,' Azim interrupts my thoughts. He indicates the other two godparents, who he introduced me to a few minutes ago. 'This is my friend Rob and I think you know Izzy, don't you?'

Emma closes her mouth, a little too hard – I worry for a second that she might have bitten her tongue – and says, 'Yes, I know Izzy, hello,' and kisses Izzy on both cheeks, before saying, 'And it's so lovely to meet you, Rob.'

She puts her hand out and Rob shakes it, and then he says, 'Hey, we're bound together for life now as fellow godparents. We need to hug.'

Emma laughs politely and says, 'You're right,' and they share a hug, while I stand there holding Thea's hand, and do my best to arrange my features into a smile.

After Emma and Rob finish their hug, Emma says, 'Hi, Callum. Lovely to see you again so soon.' She looks at Thea and says, 'Hello.'

'This is my daughter, Thea,' I say. 'Thea, this is... an old friend, Emma.' I glance at Emma and see that her features have gone a little taut. Yep. *Old friend* is a weird description, given the reality.

Then Emma smiles brightly and says, 'Hi, Thea. It's so nice to meet you.'

And then she moves herself so that Izzy is between us, and we all hover for a moment, and then Azim says, 'Becca, shall we go in?'

By unspoken but clearly mutual consent, Emma and I arrange ourselves so that Rob and Izzy are between us, and then I apply myself very hard to concentrating on the service; I don't want to be disrespectful to anyone. It's very difficult not to be hyper-aware of Emma three people away from me but I focus and say all the words in the right places and I'm pretty sure that no one will have noticed the tension between us.

* * *

After the service, we walk to the village pub for drinks and a lunch in an upstairs room.

It's easy for me to avoid Emma as we walk over en masse, because it's natural for me to walk with Thea, who has lots of questions about the christening as we wander along holding hands.

I avoid Emma very satisfactorily during the drinks, still talking to Thea plus the parents of another girl of similar age to her who she's been talking to very seriously about horses, and – as I try hard to produce some pony knowledge and not track Emma out of the corner of my eye – I'm beginning to think I'll get away with not really speaking to her.

Hopefully, on future occasions that we're both invited to, we can continue with the not-really-speaking thing until eventually the memory of this past week has receded enough into the background for us to feel moderately at ease around each other, but for now it's kind of torture.

I see Emma properly chuckle at something Rob's saying to her and feel a twinge of something that I have to admit is jealousy. I should get used to it; when and if she meets someone else, there's every chance she'll bring them to one of these occasions and I'll have to meet him and see them together.

'Daddy.' Thea's sounding stern. 'I can tell you haven't read the horse book we bought.'

'Sorry, darling. It's right at the top of my to-be-read pile.' I turn so that I can't see Emma at all and won't be distracted any more.

When Becca claps her hands and tells us it's lunchtime and that there's a seating plan, we all make our way over to the tables.

Azim and Becca have – of course – placed Emma and me next to each other.

Fortunately, Thea's on my other side, and it's always a pleasure to talk to my wonderful daughter, and Rob is on Emma's other side and seems more than delighted to spend the whole meal talking very animatedly with both Emma and Izzy, his other seat neighbour, but mainly Emma.

If I'm honest, I find Rob a little dislikeable.

The lunch is a long one.

Afterwards, we all stand up and mingle and I take Thea to chat to Becca's grandmother, before making the excuse that I promised Thea's mum that I'd get her back to London in good time so she isn't too tired before the sports camp she's doing tomorrow morning.

I say goodbye to everyone, and with Azim and Becca's eyes on us, I realise that I'm going to have to go over to say goodbye to Emma.

18

EMMA

I've seen out of the corner of my eye – which has been pointed surreptitiously in Callum's direction for the past six interminable hours – him saying goodbye to everyone.

I'm pretty sure he's going to come and say goodbye to me too; he's going to have to or people might notice.

'Emma?' Becca says.

'Yes?' I reply with extreme brightness.

'I said was the journey back with Callum a disaster? Azim and I told each other about the two of you and we thought you seemed really well suited, so if I'm being truthful we might slightly have been setting you up, but you look like you've been actively avoiding each other all day. I'm so sorry if you didn't get on during the journey. I hope it isn't too hideous being here together.'

Oh *fuck*.

Honestly, it's very annoying that Becca's such a lovely, empathetic person that she's noticed. I don't want to ruin Rose's upcoming first birthday party, which Becca's already mentioned (Rose is already nine months old; they waited for me to come back from my trip to do her christening) or any other future occasions that they want godparents at.

'No, not at all!' I exclaim. 'Callum's lovely. He was a great travel companion. He's brilliant at map reading, which was really helpful, and, yes, just really nice. Very nice.' I look at Becca and read doubt on her face and *fucking hell*. I can see very clearly what, as a good friend and godmother, I am going to have to do now.

I am going to have to have a chummy-looking conversation with Callum.

'You're right that I haven't had much opportunity to speak to him today,' I tell her. 'Izzy and I were talking to Rob for most of lunch; he's hilarious, such good company. And I think Callum was busy talking to Thea. It's obviously always special for him whenever he's able to spend time with her.'

Which is clearly true.

I'm getting into my stride now; any minute I'm going to be believing every word that comes out of my own mouth.

'Eek. I can see that Callum's leaving. Let me go and just have a quick chat with him now before he goes.'

'Yes, go, quick,' Becca says. I honestly think she believed me, thank goodness.

I make my way over to Callum, where he's standing near the door with Thea, looking in my direction, a bit rabbit-in-headlights, probably feeling exactly the way I do: we don't want to speak but we're going to have to.

He's wearing a suit, as he was the last time we said goodbye, on Tuesday, in Paris.

And just like then, he looks extremely tense, and as though he's having difficulty looking me in the eye.

He clearly clocks that I want to have an actual conversation, because he bends down to his daughter and says, 'Thea, gorgeous girl, why don't you pop over and ask Becca if you give can Rose that cuddle you wanted before we leave.'

'Okay.' Thea skips off.

'She's lovely, and so well-behaved,' I say truthfully.

Callum's demeanour lightens for a moment. 'Yeah, she is.'

I don't bother with any more pleasantries. I check that there's no one within earshot, and say, 'So the reason that I came over to speak to you is that Becca just asked me if we hated each other on the journey because she's noticed that we've basically ignored each other all day. And she's already told me that she wants godparents at Rose's first birthday and I'm guessing she might want us at other events over the years. And we can't ruin things for them. So we need to have a little happy-looking chat now so they won't feel awkward about inviting us to things.'

Callum nods. 'You're right.' He takes a deep breath and then he produces a fairly shit fake laugh and says, 'That's *hilarious*. Honestly, you and your stories.'

'What?' I hiss. 'That was *crap*. That was the fakest-looking laugh I've ever seen. And *what*? Me and my stories? Are we from the nineteen-seventies?'

'Did they say that in the nineteen-seventies?'

'I don't bloody know, do I, but they definitely don't say it in the twenty-twenties.'

'Who's they?'

'Oh, for fuck's sake.' I glare at him and then say, 'Watch this for a really good fake laugh.' And then I relax my face muscles and produce what I'm pretty sure is an *amazingly* genuine-looking laugh.

'That *was* good,' Callum concedes.

'Thank you. I am actually an excellent actress even if I say it myself.' And then, I don't know what comes over me, I think it must be the general crapness of the situation having got to me, I say, 'I can convincingly fake all *kinds* of things.'

And then Callum apparently loses his mind as much as I've lost mine, because he says, 'I'm pretty sure you weren't faking *things* this week.'

And then we stare at each other and Callum says, 'Yeah, I don't know why I said that,' and I say, 'Me neither.'

There's a long pause, during which we just carry on staring at each other, before I finish, loudly, with, 'Oh, no, such a shame that you have to leave so soon. But let's catch up in London.'

'Definitely,' Callum replies, also loudly. 'I need to introduce you to my local. Have a good journey back. Are you in the van?'

'Always,' I say.

'Great, then.'

And then he leans a bit towards me and I lean a bit towards him and we air-kiss incredibly distantly. When Callum turns and walks over to Thea, I turn and walk towards Rob and Izzy and Azim's brothers.

And that's that.

I might practise some better fake chat before the next time I'm forced to see Callum.

19

CALLUM

Three months later

Wow. I blink. I think it might take some time for my eyes to recover. I've just walked into a pink fluffy bunny alternate universe. It's Rose's first birthday party, in a church hall in Putney that's been decorated with pink and bunnies to within an inch of its life and is filled with people who have very much bought into the pink theme. Many of them have also adopted bunny motifs. I am very underdressed, in a green shirt and blue jeans, entirely bunny-free.

I wish Thea was here because I think she'd love it, but she had a party of her own to go to today so couldn't make it.

'Callum.' Becca rushes towards me carrying Rose on her hip. Rose is wearing a blue dress with pink bunnies all over it and a fluffy bunny headband thing. Given the way everyone else is dressed (some of the adults have gone full head-to-toe bunny), I'm genuinely surprised to see that Becca is not wearing any kind of rabbit costume; she's just wearing a regular (although pink) dress that you could wear in a normal, non-bunny environment. 'So lovely to see you,' she says and gestures around with her free arm. 'We have a bunny-themed party. Rose likes bunnies.'

'I would never have guessed.'

Becca rolls her eyes at me and laughs, and I immediately see why she and Emma get on so well.

Emma.

I haven't seen her since the christening and I didn't ask Azim whether she'd be here today, but I've been operating on the assumption that she will be.

That is to say: I've been periodically panicking about seeing her and then pushing all thoughts of the possible meeting out of my mind and throwing myself into work, exercise and spending time with Thea. It's almost worked. I'd say I haven't thought about her more than maybe a hundred times this week, and it's been three months since I last saw her. *Totally* over her, *totally* not missing her. *Totally* not behaving like a love-sick juvenile.

I try to scan the room without Becca noticing and I can't see Emma anywhere. I very much want to ask whether she's coming but I'm not going to.

I am not that pathetic.

Maybe Emma's one of the bunny-costumed adults. She's a loyal friend; she'd do that for Becca.

One of the bunnies is a lot shorter than the others; maybe it's her.

I'm about to casually ask who the bunnies are when Rose makes a lunge for freedom, leaping out of Becca's arms in my direction.

I catch her, laugh with her for a moment, and then put her down on the floor, and she toddles off holding Becca's hand, which is ideal as I can now scan the room more thoroughly for Emma.

My eyes have adjusted now to all the pink and fluffiness and I can't see her anywhere. I think I'm going to have to go and check whether the small bunny's her. Then I can relax and just watch the door like an obsessive hawk.

I make my way over to Azim (who's wearing a pink shirt with navy jeans but nothing bunny-related) on a route round the edge of the room that takes me past the smallest bunny. Nope, not Emma. Even though I can't see her face I just know that it isn't her; whoever this woman is, she holds herself differently.

It's always good to see Azim, and I take an immediate liking to the (pink-clad) cousins of Becca's he introduces me to.

As we chat, I position myself so that I can see the door, and as the minutes tick by, I begin to relax. I was a little bit late and perhaps three other guests have trickled in after me, but there have been no more arrivals for a while, so I don't think Emma's coming. I'm relieved. I'm also something else – maybe disappointed, I'm not sure. But mainly, I'm relieved. Definitely.

I relax so much into the conversation that when the door suddenly opens and a woman in pink hurtles through – and I realise very quickly that it's actually Emma – I physically start and almost spill my glass of (pink, naturally) prosecco.

'Sorry, sorry, very clumsy of me,' I say to Azim.

I begin to move forward towards the door, forgetting momentarily that Emma has not come here to meet me and that it isn't an automatic thing that we'll greet each other before she speaks to anyone else.

And in fact she's now surrounded by people but I've already started to approach so if I don't keep on walking towards her I'm going to draw attention to both of us and I don't think we want to do that. We don't want Azim and Becca to feel awkward inviting us to things together (Emma pointed that out to me at the christening and she was definitely right) so I just keep on walking anyway and wonder when the last time I felt this gauche was. Possibly never.

So a few seconds later I'm interrupting a group of hugging,

pink-clad women to say hello to Emma. And to all of the others. I need to greet them all, otherwise it will look weird.

'Hi, hello,' I say around the little group. A couple of the women are *very* effusive with their greetings and I wonder if I'm coming across as the kind of person who'd be on the pull at my god-daughter's first birthday party.

I eventually manage to sidle round the edge of the group to have a separate word with Emma.

'How have you been?' I immediately wonder why it was that I was so keen to speak to her in the first place, because this suddenly feels overwhelming and I just want to run for the hills. 'You look well.'

Pink suits her. *Every* colour suits her, actually.

She's wearing wide jeans and a short, pale pink jumper, and she has her beautiful thick hair up in a highish ponytail with a big pink scrunchie round it, and she has very nice pink lipstick on; she's making every woman in the room who's wearing a dress look overdressed and the few people in the room (like me) who haven't done the pink thing look like they haven't made enough effort. Basically, she looks perfect, and no one else does, because no one else is her.

Basically, I'm an infatuated idiot. What I should do, for both our sakes I'm guessing, is *not* try to start a lengthy conversation with her.

Emma looks up at me properly for the first time since I walked over and very suddenly my whole body goes cold. Her eyes look slightly damp and they only meet mine for a second before they slide away, and her features are just… frozen. She looks… stricken. And I obviously can't tell for certain but I'm pretty sure that it's seeing me that's caused her to look like this.

And all at once, I see things clearly, for the first time in twelve years.

I'm a complete idiot.

Emma's hurt. And I know that I hurt her.

I told her we couldn't be together because I didn't want to hurt her and because I didn't want to get hurt when things finished. And I believed what I said.

But she's hurt anyway. And I'm not exactly loving life at the moment. I mean, I can keep myself more than busy with Thea and work and exercise and friends, but it's only the time I'm spending with Thea when I'm really living. The rest of it, the keeping myself busy, it's like I'm just killing time. Until what? *For* what?

Emma visibly straightens and looks back into my eyes for a moment and does a half-smile. 'I see you read the dress code.'

'Yeah,' I say, relieved, because small talk is going to be a lot easier than dealing with my thoughts right now. 'I was in a rush and didn't make it past the date, time and venue. You know what's really ridiculous? I bought a new pink shirt literally the other day.'

Emma shakes her head, sorrowfully, looking a lot happier now that we're definitely talking about absolutely nothing remotely important or related to *us*. 'Rose is going to be really offended if you aren't careful. I'm not sure you're going to be her favourite godparent if you carry on like this.'

'Hey. I can be a favourite godparent.'

I am good at this. I can totally do acquaintance-style chat with Emma.

'Really. What present did you buy?' Her smile's very smug. She's definitely bought something amazing.

'In my defence, I've been very busy. *Really* busy.'

Emma mock-horrified gasps and narrows her eyes. 'Did you... give her money?'

'I mean... everyone likes money to spend?'

'Yes, I see her now on the Tube by herself next week on the way to Westfield with cash burning a hole in her pocket. Oh, no, wait, that won't be for at least another thirteen years I'd say?'

I'm not going to take this lying down. 'You scoff, but thinking of future Rose, and Azim's excellent eye for an investment, she's going to be very grateful to me when she *is* fourteen, because by then this money, and any other monetary gifts I thoughtfully give her for every single Christmas and birthday, will be worth a *lot*, and she will therefore have a *lot* of fun in Westfield in her teens courtesy of me.'

I smile triumphantly because that's a great spur-of-the-moment argument.

'I feel like one-year-olds are famously quite big into instant gratification, though?'

'Well, maybe that isn't healthy; maybe godparents should be teaching them a bit of restraint and financial prudence.'

'Oh, please. Basically, I have an amazing, *actual* present and you do not.'

I relent, because she obviously really wants to boast. 'Okay, what is your amazing present?'

Emma's smile is incredibly smug now. 'It's over there. The best one.'

I look over to the present table.

'Not...?' There's an enormous, unwrapped present, which is clearly going to be hands-down the best one of the day, given the party theme and Rose's clear preferences. It's a gigantic, incredibly fluffy pink toy bunny. It's almost as big as Emma.

'Yes,' Emma crows. 'It's clearly going to be the winner. I'm going to be the best godparent *ever*. And I will be this good every single Christmas and every single birthday, just so you know.'

I narrow my eyes. 'Are you suggesting that you genuinely believe you're going to achieve favourite godparent status?'

'I mean.' Emma spreads her hands, smug smile still in place. 'Yes?'

I give a scornful laugh. 'I wouldn't be so sure. There are other ways of being the best godparent and I'm *all* over them.'

'What are those other ways?'

I have no idea. *Obviously,* Emma is going to be the favourite godparent. She'd be the favourite in any group and she's my favourite too, because she's just perfect and gorgeous, and oh my God I am besotted with her. I love her.

Oh my God, I love her so much. I'm reeling from the magnitude of it.

'Um,' I say, trying to recover my wits, 'I can't actually divulge my secrets because you might copy them.'

'I *never* copy.'

I open my mouth to continue, because honestly, Emma and I can talk crap like this for hours and hours and I love doing it and I'm desperate to spend time with her without any stressful deep conversation, but I'm interrupted by a woman I don't know (in a bright pink all-in-one trouser-and-top garment and a bunny hairband) coming over and giving Emma an enormous hug.

'Ems,' she shrieks.

Emma hugs her back and they exclaim about how they haven't seen each other for ages and I realise that I should really bow out of the conversation now with good grace.

'I'll catch you later,' I say, before walking away in a daze.

As I go, I think about how we were great together in the summer.

Emma was great. She's always great.

And I was great insofar as I did not behave like the stupid dick I used to behave like when I was young.

I *liked* the person I was when we were travelling together.

Emma had a good effect on me, made me a better version of myself.

I've grown up, I realise. I've proved for years now that I can live well. I'm a good father to Thea.

But maybe I haven't been letting myself have fun. Maybe I've been scared that it was having fun that turned me into a complete idiot.

I had a lot of fun with Emma in the summer. The only other person I have that much fun with is Thea.

Oh my God.

I've been such an idiot.

I know what I want to do.

I want, very desperately, to talk to Emma.

She is, unfortunately, surrounded by people.

* * *

For me, the party is long, because I spend the entirety of it watching Emma while trying not to look as though I'm watching her and instead trying to look engrossed in whatever conversation I happen to be having with some other pink-clothed person.

We go full first-birthday-party.

We play games including pass the parcel and pin the tail on the donkey. Adults as well as children of all ages. (The adults are at least as competitive as the children.)

We eat a lot of pink food on pink plates with pink napkins.

'Do you think I got the theme right?' Becca asks me and Azim at one point.

'It's perfect,' Azim tells her. 'The perfect little girl's party. *You're* perfect.'

And then they exchange a quick kiss and a hug and then stand with their arms round each other's waists and I realise that I really, really, really want that with Emma. Forever.

Right now, though, we are two entirely separate people who happen to be at the same child's birthday party. We've only interacted for one conversation and could easily not speak to each other again today and will then have no reason to interact again until the next time we're at a party of Azim and Becca's. I have really messed up.

The party drags while I try to be as natural as possible chatting to different people (but not Emma because she's extremely busy the whole time with other guests). Eventually, several small and not-so-small children enter various states of meltdown, which I'm really not surprised about because the amount of sugar that's been eaten is insane – I remember Thea on the occasional sugar rush when she was younger and it wasn't pretty – and people start to make a move.

I'm talking to Azim's parents, as always with half an eye on Emma (I do not like this version of myself), when I see her hugging Becca and making for the door.

'So great to see you again.' I pump Azim's dad's hand and kiss his mum's cheek and turn and almost sprint across the hall to the exit.

There are two routes out of the churchyard, one straight ahead and one to the right. I just catch a glimpse of Emma's swishing ponytail as she disappears through the gate maybe twenty metres ahead of me. I run up the path and see that she's halfway along an alleyway to the left.

I begin to speed-walk until I'm fairly close to her, and then say, 'Emma, hi.'

'Oh, hi,' she says over her shoulder, not slowing down.

The alleyway isn't wide enough for us to walk side by side. She carries on walking, fairly fast, and I obviously don't want to overtake her because I'd like to speak to her. I'm not going to bar her way because that would be ridiculous, so I carry on walking just behind. It doesn't feel comfortable.

When we emerge onto the street, she says, 'Goodbye, then.'

'Which way are you going?' I ask.

'That way.' She points left. My car's parked to the right.

I passed my driving test last month; something about being with Emma on the trip made me think that now was the time to do it, so I took a few lessons and then regained my licence. I wanted to message her to tell her but obviously couldn't, since I'm the one who walked away. Now isn't the time, either.

'Me too,' I say and turn left with her.

Emma doesn't speak, and fair enough; we don't have to pretend now because there isn't anyone from the party in sight.

All I can think about is how much I love her.

I'd love to spend time with her. I hope she feels the same way. I don't want to rush things, though, make any more stupid mistakes.

There's a big silence between us and I'm beginning to panic that we'll reach the main road too soon and she'll just hop on a bus and be gone. I mean, I could take the bus with her, obviously, but I can hardly follow her all the way home. So I should say something.

Suddenly, words just fall out of me. 'Can we go on a date?'

I can't believe I just said that and am terrified that she'll say no, but I'm also so pleased to have asked.

Emma stops dead in the middle of the pavement and looks at me.

A young couple with a baby in a buggy dodge round us, and then Emma says, 'Sorry, what?'

'I'd love to go on a date with you if you'd like to.'

I don't feel encouraged by the expression on her face, which is kind of shocked, and maybe annoyed, definitely not a big yes-I-love-you smile or anything else positive.

'I... No.' Emma shakes her head. 'No, I can't.' She sounds pretty decisive.

'Could I ask why not?' I say, because in for a penny, in for a pound, and having asked, I'd like to know.

'I am...' She pauses and then continues, 'Never going to be able to go on a date with you.'

'Could I possibly ask why?' I repeat, promising myself that I'll have the dignity not to ask a third time.

She starts walking again, very briskly, and then after a few paces says, 'Because I got back with my ex. In Paris actually. We got engaged and so that's that really. It's over between you and me. Forever. End of. I mean, not that I'm suggesting that we ever started again. But if we had done. We'd be over. Because I'm engaged.'

Oh. God.

I had not thought of that. I am so... arrogant? Stupid? Whatever, I realise that I'd just assumed she would still be single. But there is absolutely no reason that she should be, of course. Fuck, though. And in *Paris*. Straight after we... Well, again, totally her prerogative.

'Your fiancé wasn't here today?' I sound pathetic but I really don't care.

'He's busy. Anyway, goodbye. Lovely to see you. See you at the next one.'

She walks off while I stand staring after her before turning round and trudging back to my car.

20

EMMA

I speed-walk all the way to Putney train station. The departures screen tells me that there's a Central-London-bound train approaching and I barrel my way through the barriers and down the steps and hurl myself through the nearest doors just as they're closing. The train pulls out of the station and I plonk myself onto a seat.

Anger and misery lent me wings (no bad thing because according to the screen in the station the next train wasn't for another half hour; there's a reduced Sunday service due to works on the line) but now I'm sitting down and I don't know what to do with all this emotion.

For the first time that I can remember, I feel like I want to punch something. Or some*one*. I picture myself planting a fist into Callum's face and screw my own face up. He'd probably just stand there, in man-of-steel mode, not flinching, and then come up with a one-liner that would make me laugh despite myself. I swallow a sob. I *miss* him.

I truly hate feeling like this.

Bloody Callum. I was doing okay. I was dealing with being in the same room as him. I'd probably have thought about him on the way home and felt a little miserable, but I wouldn't have felt this bad if he hadn't said what he said.

I don't want to think about him any more. I take my Kindle out of my bag and turn the screen on. I enjoyed the journey here, alternating between reading and looking out of the window, so all I need to do is get back into my book.

I'm too upset to read, though.

I give up and just stare out of the window at the buildings we're flashing past.

What am I actually upset about?

Callum asked me if I would like to go on a date with him.

Why am I upset about that?

I heave a really big out-loud sigh and the woman opposite me says, 'Are you okay, love?'

'Yes, I am. Sorry!' I do my best to stop any further sighing and to produce a smile, but I think it's more of a grimace.

I'm not okay, but I should be, actually.

I'd got to a point where I'm glad that Callum and I met again in the summer because I do feel as though I got closure... finally.

That was good. I don't want to go backwards. I want to carry on looking forwards and enjoying my definitively Callum-free life. I've moved on. He told me once and for all that we won't be together and I accepted that. I wasn't looking forward to seeing him at the party today, and it was a bit difficult, but I dealt with it and I was *fine*.

Until he asked me to go on a date.

Why did he ask? Why now? And why ask the question at all?

Maybe, actually, it wouldn't hurt to meet up with him. Maybe, actually, it would be a good thing because now it feels like I need to get closure again rather than wondering for ages why he asked me.

It might be upsetting seeing him but it *would* probably be better than having ongoing nagging questions.

We draw into Vauxhall, and the woman opposite me stands to get off.

As she passes me, she says, 'Whatever it is, love, it'll be okay.'

I manage to smile at her. 'You're very wise.'

'I know.' She grins at me before getting off.

I open my bag and take out my phone and send Callum a message saying:

> I lied.

21

CALLUM

I'm in a huge rush to make it to pick Thea up from her party on time because I stayed at Azim and Becca's for longer than I should have done, waiting for Emma to leave so that I could make a gigantic arse of myself asking her out.

Marvellous all round.

I think about Emma for the entire journey.

I'm *gutted* that she got back with her ex.

They got back together in Paris. In fucking Paris. Right after I walked out of her life. The night after our last perfect evening together.

I don't think I'm being arrogant to feel that it's entirely my fault, that we could be together now if I hadn't walked away at that point.

I am the most stupid person I've ever met.

I just threw away an opportunity to be happy.

Well, there we go. I was thinking back there that I've grown up and that maybe I no longer wreck things. Wrong, clearly.

I really hope Emma's happy.

Maybe this is for the best. For her, anyway. And I do very much want her to be very happy.

Okay. I am not going to fuck up and be late for Thea on top of the Emma debacle.

* * *

Having taken every back route and cheeky dodge that I know of and crossed London in record time, I squeeze the car into a parking space a ten-minute walk from the party, and sprint, arriving only a couple of minutes late.

That's definitely my biggest win of the day so far, and it's made even better when Thea, on sight of me, breaks into a huge smile. I might be a complete idiot but my daughter loves me and I got here for her, and in this moment not a lot else counts.

I'm taking her for pizza before returning her to her mum in time for her to get an earlyish night before school tomorrow morning. I have a rule that I won't look at my phone when I'm eating with her and I'm certainly not going to be breaking it this evening because I don't want to fuck up anything else in my life.

As we approach the pizza place, my phone vibrates. Maybe it's Emma.

I'm *so* pissed off about her getting back with her ex. It didn't really occur to me that she'd have a partner. But why wouldn't she? What an arrogant, stupid idiot I've been. I wonder if that message *was* from her. No, of course it wasn't.

After I've parked and we're getting out of the car, I take a cursory glance at my screen; I'll read and reply to any messages when I've said goodbye to Thea later but I can't help wanting to confirm that Emma hasn't for some reason been in touch.

One message – from Emma – stands out.

I lied.

What? I can't drag my eyes away from the screen. My fingers are literally itching to reply to ask what she means.

'Daddy, are we going?'

God. I'm not jeopardising my relationship with Thea in any way, including in ignoring her so that I can attempt to sort out my messed-up not-a-relationship with Emma.

'Sorry, Thea.' I push my phone into my pocket and lock the car.

I can't help wondering, though, as we walk to the restaurant, what Emma means. She lied about what?

'Daddy, can I have dough balls *and* garlic bread?'

I laugh and say, 'Only if you share with me.'

I'll ask Emma later. Not now.

I force my attention from thoughts of Emma to Thea and as always have a great evening with my daughter.

To my shame, though, after I've hugged her goodnight on her mum's doorstep, I don't even wait until I'm back in the car before pulling my phone out and opening Emma's message.

I type as I walk along the pavement:

> What did you lie about?

I get into the car and sit at the wheel for several minutes, waiting for Emma's reply, but there's nothing, so eventually I just drive home.

For the next couple of hours, I pounce on my phone every time it vibrates, until finally, as I'm getting ready for bed, I get a reply from Emma.

> I didn't get back with my ex.

My eyebrows nearly hit my hair. Oh my God.
That's huge. Gigantic.

I'm smiling, I realise, just because she did not in fact get back with her ex. Does that make me a bad person?

I have a lot of questions.

Why did she lie about it this afternoon? And why is she telling me the truth now?

I wish we were in the same place because it would be a lot easier to gauge things face to face. And also, I'd really love to just be with her again, but that's nothing new.

> Why did you tell me that you did?

I type, and then delete it because it sounds curt and aggressive. I think hard for quite a long time, and then write:

> Are you okay?

I stare at my words for a bit and eventually decide that that's the best I'm going to come up with, and send the message.

Emma replies almost immediately, while I'm still holding my phone, staring at it as though that will have some telepathic effect.

Her text says:

> I'm a little confused.

I write:

> What are you confused about?

I send it immediately before I can waste more minutes wondering whether it's the right thing to say and possibly causing her to get bored and effectively end the conversation.

> I'm confused about why you would ask me to go on a date.

I type:

> It's because I love you.

But then I delete my words in a panic, because that doesn't seem a sensible thing to say. Or maybe it would be. I don't know.

I want to write *something*, though, because otherwise the conversation might end.

In the end, I write:

> Would you be happy to meet me so I can tell you?

Now Emma's typing and deleting and typing and deleting and then... nothing.

Fuck. Maybe asking her to meet was too pushy. And – of course; metaphorical head slap – I now realise that the reason she lied is probably that she really doesn't want to go on a date with me because she's moved on and that was the first excuse that came into her head.

Okay. I'm going to brush my teeth.

The second I stand up, leaving my phone on the table, I hear it buzz.

In response to my question about whether she'd be happy to meet, Emma has written:

> I think so.

Fuck me. I literally punch the air and then, with incredible restraint, write:

> Great. When are you free?

There's a pause and then she says:

> Maybe Saturday afternoon?

I reply:

> Perfect.

I was supposed to be going away for the weekend with friends. I'll have to join them on Saturday evening.

I really want to send Emma another message telling her that I love her, but sanity prevails, and I just type:

> Let me know where you'd like to meet and when.

I feel like a kid of Thea's age waiting for Christmas Day. I already know that this week is going to drag. Oh my *God* I'm excited. I feel as though this is my one remaining chance – forever – with Emma.

I do not want to mess it up.

22

EMMA

On Saturday, when I arrive at the café near Alexandra Palace where I'm meeting Callum, the first thing I do is look at my watch. I'm fifteen minutes early.

I have no idea what length of journey he'll have to get here because I have no idea where he lives, which is utterly ridiculous given that we were literally joined at the hip for a good week only three months ago.

I turn to walk back out and maybe wander round some shops for the next twenty minutes and then I remember that I'm an adult and that if I were meeting a girlfriend now I'd just sit down and read or do something on my phone. I'm not a love-sick, trying-to-play-hard-to-get teenager. Well, I'm kind of love-sick. But the rest of it: no. I'm going to behave like the adult I supposedly am.

I go in and find a table in the corner of the room and sit down. And this is good. Very good. Fine.

On Sunday I was tempted to ask Callum if he was free to meet on Monday. In fact, I'd have happily met him at in the middle of the night then and there. But also, I wouldn't have done; having been bitten before I do feel cautious. If there's any possibility of us rekindling something it needs to happen slowly and it needs to happen right.

I decided that it would be better to wait a week, just in case seeing me in person last weekend swayed him but, on reflection, he decided he regretted suggesting a date. Because if there's one thing about Callum telling me he loves me and then walking away, it's that it's a shit experience that I do not want to repeat any more.

That's why I told him that I'd got back with Dev; I was panicking and I wanted to say something that would mean he wouldn't ask me ever again.

I did consider Dev's suggestion for a long moment in the museum, but then I thought about how very much I loved Callum and just knew that I couldn't do it to Dev; it would be unfair not being able to offer him my whole heart.

I order a latte and a glass of tap water and then I get my Kindle out.

I sit and read (I say read, I stare at the screen and do not take any of the words in) and look at the door at the same time.

When Callum arrives, I see him immediately.

Again, I have the instincts of a teenage idiot: I'm very tempted to pretend to be incredibly engrossed in my Kindle.

I am, however, as I have already reminded myself a few times this afternoon, an adult, and I do not want to behave like an idiot.

So I put my Kindle back in my bag and smile at him as he crosses the room towards me.

My heart's beating at a hundred miles an hour. Callum's wearing worn-in jeans and a navy quarter-zip jumper under a jacket and I can't imagine anyone ever looking better in any clothes ever. I noticed last week that he hasn't bothered recently with the super-tidy haircut that he had in the summer; his lovely thick hair's curling over his collar and it very much suits him. His eyes are fixed on me and his smile seems personally targeted, as though

I'm the only person in the vicinity, even though he actually has to step over a couple of toddlers and dodge round several other people to reach me.

I stay seated when he gets to the table, really because I don't know how to physically greet him. If I don't hug him, maybe that would be odd. But if I do, maybe that would be odd too. Basically, I'm not sure where we're at hug-wise.

He hovers for a second and then pulls the chair opposite me out. He sits down and leans his arms on the table.

'Hi,' he says, as my stupid mind fixates on the obvious latent strength in his forearms and how much I like his hands.

'Hi.'

'Thank you for agreeing to meet.' He sounds very formal.

'It's nice to see you.' I'm just as polite.

'Would you like to order something?' the woman who served me asks him.

'An espresso would be great, thank you.'

The woman simpers a little under the force of Callum's smile (to be fair it's truly lovely) and then leaves us to it.

We sit there in silence for a long moment and I begin to wonder whether there was actually any point in us meeting today. We're good at small talk, but I think we have to do more than that now. I have nothing beyond inanities to offer, and to my disappointment Callum doesn't seem to be rushing into explaining himself. Perhaps we'll have a half hour of careful chat and then just go our separate ways.

I'm beginning to feel very disappointed – I couldn't help hoping that he might say something big – but then, just as I'm about to comment on the unusually wide range of cakes available here, Callum suddenly says, all in a rush, 'The reason I asked you to meet is that I wanted to apologise for my incredible stupidity and tell you that I love you and I've never stopped loving you, and

I wanted to ask you again if you'd be happy to go on a date with me.'

'Um.' I'm frowning, trying to interpret what he just said.

'I'm sorry,' he says, after a while.

I nod, for no good reason. My brain's still struggling to process his words.

'Could you explain?' I ask eventually.

'Of course. I mean, I can try.'

I wait.

'Basically.' He stops and while I'm waiting for him to carry on I watch his face. I love the shape of his jaw. 'I have always loved you. The day we met, the moment you resigned from the café and then immediately gave me this huge, gleeful smile, I was just hit with this incredible certainty that you were the girl I needed to marry one day. Like, I just wanted to be with you and make you happy forever. Obviously, I didn't actually know you at *all* at that point, but as we got to know each other I just loved you more and more. It was as though on that first day an artist had painted on a canvas an outline of love, and as I got to know you the middle of the love shape got filled in.'

I sniff and wipe under my eyes. Callum's rarely poetic like this, and it's gorgeous. Also, now he says it, that's exactly how it happened for me too. The filling-in-details thing.

'Obviously, though,' he continues, 'I was – as we both know – wild. When I proposed and you told me that I needed to sort myself out, you were right. And as I told you before, I intended to get my life back on track and then go back to you, but in the end I didn't. And then fast-forward to when we met again in Italy, and clearly, from my side, the love had never gone, and I stupidly, while thinking I knew that we shouldn't be together, allowed myself to fall into that week-long romance with you. And then I told you that

I didn't think we could ever be together because I thought I'd hurt you again.'

'Yes?' I encourage, because finally we're getting to *now*, and he's bloody stopped talking.

'Last weekend at the party, I don't know,' he says, finally getting going again, 'I just felt – and I could be wrong; I could be the most arrogant idiot in the world and please tell me if that's the case – that you looked as though the sight of me made you hurt and I just suddenly thought that if us not being together hurt you what was the point in me saying let's not be together in order not to hurt you? If that makes sense.'

'You're an idiot,' I state.

Callum nods.

I look into his eyes and see fear there.

I want to tell him that I love him but right now I can't do that.

'So, were we to go on a date,' I say, 'how would you like to see things progress from here?'

'I would like... I'd like us to be together. Properly. I love you.'

'I see.'

I want to allow myself to be happy but given everything that's happened between us in the past I'm nervous.

'In the summer, it was all very surface-level,' I tell him. 'I realised after you left Paris that there were signs, which, if I hadn't been actively trying to avoid seeing them, I would have realised were practically slapping me in the face.'

Callum nods again, slowly.

'For example,' I say, 'all our conversations. They were very superficial. All small talk, banter. No details. Neither of us knows where the other one lives. I don't think you even know what job I do unless you've googled me. I definitely didn't tell you, because we didn't go there. And that's *so* superficial. And we didn't even get that far.'

'That's true,' Callum agrees. 'And it was my fault, wasn't it? You tried to move the conversation there a couple of times and I blocked you.'

'Yep.'

We sit in silence for a few moments, and then Callum says, 'Could I ask a question? Obviously please do feel very free to not answer.'

'Okay.'

'What job *do* you do?'

I look hard at him, into his lovely, still-fearful eyes, and then down at his hands, which he's fisted so hard that his knuckles are showing white.

It's the eyes and the knuckles that do it.

'I'm a special needs teacher,' I say.

'Do you… work locally?' he asks tentatively.

'The school's in Muswell Hill. It's a primary school.' I decide to tell him more, to see if he reciprocates. I don't feel good about the fact that I feel as though I'm testing him, but also, I kind of need to. 'I live near Bowes Park in a flat.'

'Do you enjoy it?' He's still sounding very cautious, as though he's dealing with an unpredictable wild animal or something.

'Yep. It's obviously challenging but it's very rewarding.'

'How did you manage to get the time for your trip?' He's still speaking slowly, as though he's very keen to ask the questions and hear the answers, but nervous about how I might react. Fair enough, because while I *did* want to talk about this stuff with him before, I'm not so sure now. Especially given that I *still* know nothing about his current life other than the broad fact that he's a lawyer.

'I took a term's unpaid sabbatical and ran it into my summer holiday.' I don't want to talk about myself any more if he isn't going to talk to me about himself, so I ask, 'What about you?'

He flexes his hands a little. 'I work for a large law firm in the City. I do actually quite enjoy it. I live in a flat in Fulham but I'm in the process of buying a house so there's more space for Thea when she's with me. I have her on alternate weekends. I'm on perfectly amicable terms with her mum. When she isn't staying with me, I see her one day on the weekend and once a week on a weeknight, usually Wednesdays.'

He pauses, and then says, 'I've been very keen to be as hands-on and involved as possible so that I'm a completely different kind of parent from mine. Obviously, Thea wasn't planned but from the moment Leona, her mum, told me about her I just wanted to be the best dad I possibly could. My parents were shit. They didn't turn up for school concerts or sports days. They only cared when I succeeded at something, and then really only – from where I was standing – to boast about it to their friends and colleagues. If I was upset about something, they never knew, so I have no idea whether they would have attempted to help or not, but I suspect not. I don't want to be that kind of father. I feel like I have no role model, but I'm doing my best, and so far so good.

'On Wednesday I had one of the proudest moments of my life. Thea told me all about a bully in her class who's been victimising one of Thea's friends, and then told me that I'm the best dad in the world because she can tell me anything and I always listen. I don't think there's any higher compliment than that.'

'That's so gorgeous,' I say. 'I'm so pleased for you.'

'Thank you. I worried for quite a long time that at some point I'd turn into an uncaring parent but then I suddenly realised one day – Thea's fifth birthday in fact – that it would already have happened, and I relaxed. And obviously I'm sure I make my mistakes but I'm pretty sure she knows I love her. And that's huge.'

'That *is* huge. You sound like an amazing dad.'

'Thank you,' he says again. He opens his mouth and then closes it.

'What?' I say. And then: 'No, you don't need to tell me. Sorry.'

'No, no, it's just I *was* going to say something and then I thought better of it in case it sounded very manipulative. I mean it was true, what I was going to say, but maybe it would sound as though I was saying it on purpose.'

Callum is *never* this uncertain. It's weird. Also cute.

'Just say it,' I say. 'If you want to? And I will bear in mind that you are not being manipulative?'

'I mean, basically I was just going to say that I *never* talk about this stuff. With anyone. But I wanted to tell you.'

He's right; it could have sounded manipulative. But it doesn't. And I feel that I've just received something very precious. Even when we were together when we were young he didn't talk about his parents much.

'Thank you,' I say for the umpteenth time.

'No, thank *you*.'

We sit there for a long time, just kind of looking at each other, and then the café owner places Callum's coffee in front of him and says, 'So sorry it took so long.'

'Not at all, thank you.' He glances at the woman for a second and flashes her a smile and then switches his gaze back to me, as though he can't bear to look away for too long.

We resume the mutual gazing. I don't know what to say now and maybe Callum feels the same way.

'Cake?' I say eventually.

'Sorry?'

'I wondered if you thought it would be nice to get some cake.'

'Oh, yes. Absolutely. Cake would be great.'

'Good. What kind?'

'Whatever you like? Unless we aren't sharing?'

'I'm easy either way.'

'Me too.'

'What's your *favourite* cake?' I ask.

'Not a big cake eater.'

'You could get a different snack? Or nothing? We could have no cake?'

'Honestly, whatever you prefer.'

I begin to snigger. 'This is a ridiculous conversation.'

'Yeah, too polite,' Callum agrees.

'Yes.'

'And a little awkward too.'

'Yes.'

'So.' He suddenly looks very serious. 'To get it back out there: no obligation at all, obviously, but I wondered if you would like to go for a date.'

His knuckles are white again.

This time it's an easy decision.

'One date would be very nice.' I reach out and touch his hand briefly and he catches my fingers and I get the most enormous thrill, right up my arm and through my whole body. 'Just one date for now. A real *first* date. And then just see what happens. If anything.'

I cannot risk too much heartbreak with Callum again. I can't leap straight into happily-ever-after fantasies this time. My heart can't take any more bruising.

'That sounds perfect,' Callum says.

'So basically we're going to take things very, very slowly and talk more openly and only... do stuff if we feel some level of commitment.'

'Perfect.' He pauses and then says, 'I mean, if we're going to wait to do stuff until we've talked, I can give you my entire life history right now?'

'Callum!' I glare at him.

'Sorry, joke, joke, joke.'

'A very bad one.'

'Yeah, sorry.' He grins at me and I smile back. 'Soooo... When... would you like to have that date?'

I'm suddenly feeling very decisive.

'We're both here now? We could have that cake—' I feel like if Callum is going to date me properly he's going to need to know all about my love of lemon drizzle '—and then go for a walk? I have a couple of hours free now and then I have a Zumba class and then I'm going out with girlfriends from work.'

It feels perfect that I have other plans later on. Yes, obviously I know how amazing our nights were when we were on the trip, but I really, really don't want to take things insanely fast, because if there's any hope of us going long term I think we *have* to take things slowly now, and it's ideal if there's something stopping me from giving in to any temptation.

'Great,' he says.

And then we sit and smile at each other. Callum nudges my ankle with his under the table and, honestly, I feel as though my heart's going to lift right out of my body.

EPILOGUE
EMMA

Eighteen months later

'I have a birthday surprise for you,' I tell Callum when he opens his front door to me at the beginning of the May bank holiday weekend.

'I want to say that a surprise sounds lovely but I'm remembering last time, plus you're acting very shiftily,' he says.

He's referring to when I helped Thea sign him up for her carers-and-daughters school play, *Macbeth*, as a surprise. He landed the role of Third Tree and his green face paint didn't come off properly for a good fortnight.

'Not *shifty*,' I reply, 'just...' Yeah, shifty. Callum isn't the *biggest* fan of Miranda. One too many inconvenient breakdowns in the last year. 'Are you ready?'

Callum locks up and follows me along the road and round the corner to where I parked Miranda out of sight.

'Noooo,' he moans when he sees her.

'Callum!' I exclaim, mock-outraged. 'Are you saying you don't enjoy spending time in her with me?'

'Not at all. I love you and I love Miranda. It's just the breakdowns.'

'There won't be any,' I say confidently. 'But I've come prepared just in case.'

'You have a car mechanic tucked away in the boot?'

'No, even better, I've borrowed a tent from Samira. So on the very slim off-chance that we do break down, we can just set up home wherever we are.'

'That sounds wonderful,' Callum tells me, rolling his eyes. 'I've always wanted to sleep next to a motorway lay-by.'

'Also,' I say, deciding to ignore his annoying Miranda-related negativity (which he terms pragmatism), 'I have a *very* good playlist for you *and* I know some of the actual words. *And* I'm wearing shoes, not flip-flops.'

'*Now* you're talking.' Callum opens the passenger door and hops straight in.

A few months ago he offered to put me on his car insurance and I said no thank you because the power of his Audi terrifies me. And then I politely offered to put him on my van insurance and he very impolitely said that he was very grateful for the gesture and no offence but he'd rather get a bus, train or any other mode of transport including walking barefoot over glass.

Two hours later, we've sung a lot of Abba (to which I genuinely do know quite a lot of the words) and we've moved on to a lot of songs to which I do not know the words and to which I'm forced to sing *la* while Callum tries to drown me out with the actual words, and we are *still in London*.

'In hindsight,' Callum says, 'I wonder whether we should perhaps have left at a different time.' There's a train strike and it's full rush hour and apparently the *whole* of London is heading west like us for the weekend.

'I always enjoy journeys with you,' I say truthfully.

'Me too, actually,' Callum says. 'Even the really bad ones, and that's a compliment.' It is. He still hates traffic jams. 'And if I'm honest, I'm still grateful to Miranda for getting us back together.'

'Me too.' I'm beaming.

We eventually crawl out of the traffic jam and onto some more open roads and soon we're flying along at a heady forty-eight miles an hour.

'Referring back to our earlier conversation,' Callum says, 'what's great about loving journeys in Miranda is that they go on for so incredibly long when we go at this speed. You do know the limit here is seventy?'

'Every time,' I say.

He can't help himself. He knows I won't actually speed up. I actually think he'd be terrified if I did because one thing about Miranda is that she really is quite rickety and if there's even the tiniest of breezes you do feel as though you're going to topple over.

We reach the pub I've booked for tonight quite a lot later than expected so it's dark and we've missed dinner. (We had service station sushi instead – one day past its use-by date – genuinely quite nice, and Callum's obviously in a very good mood because he didn't mention possible food poisoning once.)

The dark doesn't totally disguise the rubbish piled up around the pub's front door, though, and all the peeling paint on the exterior.

'Is this definitely the right pub?' I ask doubtfully.

'You booked it?' Callum reminds me.

'It looked a lot more well-kept than this in the pictures. And it won Pub of the Year.'

'In 1998.' Callum points to a partially torn poster next to the door. 'I'm sure it's lovely inside, though.' He reaches above my head to push the door open and we go in together.

Five minutes later, we've been shown the chipped avocado

bathroom (very smelly and shared with the landlord) and are standing just inside our bedroom door, both jaw-dropped.

'What are you thinking?' asks Callum eventually.

'Erm. I'm not sure whether the stains, the flies or the moth traps are the biggest highlight. I'm thinking it's lucky I brought that tent.'

'I think you're right.'

Two minutes later, we're back in the car park, having left the room key on the bar.

'I'm genuinely pleased to see Miranda,' Callum tells me.

'*Finally* you recognise her worth.' I beam at him and we share a quick hug and a kiss, which is as nice as always.

As I turn the key in the driver's door, so that we can drive somewhere a little more scenic to pitch the tent, something makes me look down. And oh.

'We have a *really* flat tyre,' I tell him.

'Fortunately,' he says immediately, 'I would very, very happily treat us to a taxi and a night in a luxury hotel as a birthday present to myself.'

'That does sound good,' I concede. 'The only thing is…'

Callum looks hard at me in the glare of the streetlight above our heads. 'Are you about to tell me that Miranda's going to feel lonely?'

'No?' I lie.

'I love you,' he says. 'I'm sure we can get her towed to join us at the hotel.'

I *love* that he now calls her *her*.

* * *

Forty-five minutes later, we're in a truly lovely en-suite bedroom in a truly lovely hotel and the RAC have assured us that Miranda's on her way to the hotel car park.

'I kind of feel guilty about the first hotel,' I say, sinking onto the extremely comfortable bed, 'but also I don't because this one is *gorgeous* and I don't think I'd have booked it.'

'Exactly. Everything happens for a reason.'

'Funny you should mention that,' I segue very badly. 'Because I have a present for you. Well, two.' First, I pull out the nice jumper I've bought for him.

'Oh, wow, thank you. I *love* it,' he tells me between kisses after he's opened it.

'Now the second one,' I say, wriggling away.

'It's a box,' he says once he has the wrapping paper off.

'Yes. Happy birthday. *Open* the box.'

He opens it and looks at the key inside.

After the first few months where we took things *very* slowly, we (I) allowed ourselves to get much more involved in each other's lives – first we introduced each other properly to each other's friends and then I began to get to know Thea, who is just adorable – and now we spend a lot of evenings, nights and breakfasts together, but until now I've resisted the key exchange thing.

I'm not really sure why, actually, because Callum's the most wonderful father, and there's no way he'd have been so keen to introduce me to Thea if he hadn't viewed us – me and him – as a long-term couple, and I do trust that he isn't going to scarper again. In fact, if he asked me now, I'd definitely say yes to a key swap. I think he just asked me a tiny bit too soon and then hasn't wanted to again, maybe for fear of rejection.

'It's a key to my flat.' I'm suddenly a bit nervous. 'If you'd like it.'

'Oh my God, Emma, wow, yes I would. Thank you. That's a fantastic present.' He reaches for me and I move into his arms. I'm expecting a very long kiss but to my disappointment, Callum draws back quite quickly.

And then he says, 'Great minds,' and pulls a key from his back pocket.

'Oh my goodness,' I say. 'Your house? Oh wow. Thank you. We *are* both great minds.'

Obviously, we kiss, and, obviously, one thing leads to another and it turns out that post-key-swapping sex is *very* good.

Afterwards, as we lie in a very lovely tangle of limbs, Callum says, 'If I had more willpower, I'd have mentioned this before now, or I'd wait because there's probably a better time, but I actually can't wait.'

He reaches to the floor where our clothes are strewn and fishes around for a moment, before pulling something out of his jeans pocket.

Then he says, 'It doesn't feel right doing this naked,' and performs an impressive manoeuvre with the bed clothes, extracting a sheet that he then wraps around his waist, while I prop myself up on my elbows.

And *then* he goes down on one knee and, while my mind goes OMG-OMG-OMG-OMG-OMG, he clears his throat and says, 'Emma Milligan, will you marry me?'

I'm immediately overwhelmed by the flood of happiness that washes over my entire body and I can't speak, all I can do is literally tremble.

And then Callum stands up and says, 'No, of course not, sorry I didn't want to rush you and I totally understand given everything else that happened in the past that it might be too soon or you might never want to and don't worry and I can return the ring and this isn't an actual engagement ring anyway because I thought if we did get engaged you'd probably want to choose one together, so

I just bought one that I liked that you could wear on another finger if you liked it but don't worry, and it's fine, please don't feel bad.'

I reach up and pull him towards me so hard that he falls on top of me and then I'm hugging him as hard as I can.

'You don't need to pity-hug me,' he says.

'I'm not pity-hugging you, you *muppet*,' I say. 'I'm love-hugging you. I would love to marry you. I would *adore* to marry you. Thank you so much for asking me. I love you more than words can say and I was just so happy I couldn't speak.'

'That is possibly the biggest relief of my life,' he says.

And then he slides the ring onto the middle finger of my right hand and we just lie next to each other, gazing at each other, both of us just *beaming*.

'I think this is the most perfect moment of my life,' I whisper eventually. 'The journey to get here was more than worth it.'

'Me too.' And then Callum kisses me again, extremely thoroughly, and I feel like the luckiest woman in the world.

ACKNOWLEDGEMENTS

I've loved writing Emma and Callum's story, and am enormously grateful for the help I've had throughout.

Huge thanks to my agent, Sarah Hornsley at PFD, for all her support and advice, and to the team at Boldwood, who as always have been truly lovely. Emily Yau is an amazing editor, who I love working with. Thank you also to the wonderful Helena Newton for copyedits, Rachel Sargeant for proofreading and Clare Stacey for the beautiful cover.

And, of course a big thank you to my family and friends, for holidays together (visiting Italy and France on the page with Emma and Callum was so much fun, and it brought back lots of happy memories!), and to my husband and children for everything! A particular thank you to Annie, Claudie, Florence, Anne and Mélanie for holidays in France. I'm very grateful to you all!

And finally, thank you so much to my readers for reading!

ABOUT THE AUTHOR

Jo Lovett is the bestselling author of contemporary rom-coms including The House Swap. Shortlisted for the Comedy Women in Print Award, she lives in London.

Sign up to Jo Lovett's mailing list for news, competitions and updates on future books.

Follow Jo on social media:

facebook.com/JoLovett-Turner
x.com/JoLovettWrites

ALSO BY JO LOVETT

Another Time, Another Place

Can You Keep A Secret?

We Were on a Break

LOVE NOTES
LOVE IN EVERY CHAPTER

WHERE ALL YOUR ROMANCE
DREAMS COME TRUE!

THE HOME OF BESTSELLING
ROMANCE AND WOMEN'S
FICTION

WARNING:
MAY CONTAIN SPICE

SIGN UP TO OUR
NEWSLETTER

https://bit.ly/Lovenotesnews

Boldwood

Boldwood Books is an award-winning fiction publishing company seeking out the best stories from around the world.

Find out more at www.boldwoodbooks.com

Join our reader community for brilliant books, competitions and offers!

Follow us

@BoldwoodBooks

@TheBoldBookClub

Sign up to our weekly deals newsletter

https://bit.ly/BoldwoodBNewsletter

Printed in Great Britain
by Amazon